"Let me explain it to you."

Lord Harleston sounded more confident than he felt.

"What I propose is for you to assume the identity of a Frenchwoman, a widow. But of an Englishman, you see. You will be returning to your husband's estates in England."

Susan hesitated before posing any more arguments. "But won't it appear strange, even so, for me to be travelling alone?"

"Oh, you will not be alone," he assured her. "I have plans for your retinue."

Something about his innocent expression made her laugh. "All right, my lord. And of whom shall this retinue consist?"

"As luck would have it," he said, "my man found a young English servant who cannot return to London unless someone engages her."

Susan's tender heart was touched. "By all means, we must assist her."

"And of course," he continued, "you will need a groom."

"Of course," agreed Susan. "But who?"

Lord Harleston took a deep breath. "I shall be the groom."

"But, Lord Harleston," Susan began, "the risk—"

"I'm afraid I must insist upon it, Miss Johnstone. And as your faithful servant and groom you must call me Tom," he said with more than a touch of humour.

"Very well, *Lord* . . . Tom."

Their combined laughter brightened the gloomy little room in Calais.

Books by Patricia Wynn

HARLEQUIN REGENCY ROMANCE
  THE PARSON'S PLEASURE
12–SOPHIE'S HALLOO

Don't miss any of our special offers. Write to us at the
following address for information on our newest releases.

Harlequin Reader Service
901 Fuhrmann Blvd., P.O. Box 1397, Buffalo, NY 14240
Canadian address: P.O. Box 603,
Fort Erie, Ont. L2A 5X3

LORD TOM
PATRICIA WYNN

Harlequin Books

TORONTO • NEW YORK • LONDON
AMSTERDAM • PARIS • SYDNEY • HAMBURG
STOCKHOLM • ATHENS • TOKYO • MILAN

To my own Tom

Published April 1990

ISBN 0-373-31124-9

CHAPTER ONE

"FETCH ME THE LIGHT, confound it!"

Thomas, Lord Harleston, third Baron Harleston, stood rubbing his sore head and squinting balefully up at the sign upon which he had just bumped it. There was little moon that night and the streetlights of Calais, unlike those of London, could hardly be said to exist. The doorways, too, were poorly suited to his more than six feet of height, and the faded board which had accosted him had been nearly invisible in the darkness. But now with the aid of a lantern passed to him by the postboy and held above his head, his lordship began to make out its faded lettering. The light gleamed upon his pomaded locks, which were startlingly blond for a man of two and thirty, and shed a softer glow by which he could make out a name. M. Renard, Proprietor, he read. He lowered the lantern and returned it to the boy, telling him to wait.

Lord Harleston hesitated a moment more before knocking, questioning the lateness of the hour. This must be the shop, he reflected. The name Renard corresponded to the signature on the message he had received from Captain Johnstone just two days before in Paris. He had been on diplomatic assignment to the newly restored monarchy following the battle of Waterloo when the note came. It had not revealed much, but the appeal was clear. Frowning now, he wondered what misfortune had brought the old beau to this modest dwelling, but reminding himself of the urgent tone of the letter, he waited no longer, but lifted his hand to the shuttered door and knocked.

After a short wait, a narrow shaft of light pierced the darkness and two spectacled eyes peered out from beneath a night cap. Seeing that he had roused the shop's owner from his sleep, Lord Harleston quickly gave his name and was gratified by the result. The door was flung open wide and he was greeted with tangible relief.

"Ah, my Lord Harleston! Come in, come in!" cried Monsieur Renard. "This is wonderful! I had feared— but you are come in time. How happy will be Captain Johnstone to see you."

The bookseller's words confirmed the young man's unwelcome suspicions. "In time?" he repeated. But the fact that the note had been dictated to Renard had alerted him to the captain's condition.

Monsieur Renard's eyes lost their gleam. "Yes," he answered. "I fear that Captain Johnstone will not be with us much longer. He is without the strength to hold a pen, as I told you in my letter. I had feared he would not last until today—he scarcely interests himself in his toilette—but I am certain that your visit will do much to restore him."

To anyone not familiar with the captain's ways, this last remark might have had little meaning, but Lord Harleston understood instantly. He smiled reassuringly.

"I will do all in my power to make him comfortable. But before I go up—he *is* residing over your shop, I take it—will you be so good as to tell me what brought him here?"

"But of course," said Monsieur Renard, recalling himself. "You have not seen the captain for some time, I comprehend."

"No," Lord Harleston agreed. "He sold out after Badajoz in the Peninsula. Debts of honour," he explained. The old bookseller smiled wryly. "I have not seen him since then, although I've wondered frequently if he managed to restore his fortune once back in England."

Monsieur Renard shook his head sadly. "No, my lord. Oh, once, perhaps twice, he won heavily at the table. It was enough to stay his creditors for a while. But in the end there was no money and no one left to assist him. When all was lost, he came to me."

Lord Harleston looked at Monsieur Renard curiously. But it was not the captain's ill fortune which surprised him. Captain Johnstone, he remembered fondly, although charming, always had lived beyond his means. He was a gamester and an unlucky one, and something of a dandy besides. When in uniform, he had looked the very picture of elegance. His fob, his snuffbox, his rings were ever the finest, his exquisite linen the cleanest in the corps. Even in the thick of battle he had managed to look dressed to an inch. It was inevitable that such costly living should outrun his meagre fortune, and when it did, he had sold out. But Monsieur Renard's role in helping an English captain so soon after the cessation of hostilities—that was the puzzle.

"It was good of you," his lordship commented.

But Monsieur Renard waved a dismissive hand. "It was nothing, my lord. A long story and I must not waste your time. You must go to him. But I will tell you that I owe my life to Captain Johnstone. I would not refuse him anything and this—" he made another gesture of dismissal "—is nothing in comparison."

Lord Harleston nodded. "It is the same for me. He was my first commanding officer, you see. If it had not been for him at Ciudad Rodrigo—" He did not finish, but Monsieur Renard looked relieved.

"I see. And I was worrying that you might not care to help him. I see that I needn't have. Now," he said, turning briskly and leading Lord Harleston through the darkness to the back of the shop, "you must go up to him. I heard footsteps a moment ago so you will not be rousing them entirely and there is really no time to delay. Knock at the first door on the left at the head of the stairs and I am certain he will see you."

"A moment, *monsieur*," said the baron. Monsieur Renard turned at the sound of his voice. "You must tell me how long he has been here so that I may better repay you."

The old shopkeeper looked confused for a moment before, light dawning, he assumed an air of grave dignity. "You misunderstand, my lord," he said. "It was not to repay me that you were called. Nor was it to assume the care of Captain Johnstone. The captain knows that I shall care for him until there is no longer a need. But there is a matter which I have not the power to resolve and it is for that you are needed. Please," he said, holding up a hand and relaxing into a smile as Lord Harleston began to apologize, "go to the captain. He will explain himself to you." Monsieur Renard indicated the staircase with a gracious motion of the hand.

Abashed, but with curiosity now added to his concern, Lord Harleston mounted the stairs and, remembering his host's instructions, knocked on the first door. After a short wait, to his great surprise, the door was cracked open to reveal the figure of a young woman.

"Pardon me," he said in French, momentarily confused. "I must have made an error. I was looking for Captain Johnstone. Mademoiselle ... Renard?" She opened the door wider now and in the dim light he could see the young lady's face.

"I am Miss Johnstone," she said in perfect English.

"Miss Johnstone?" Lord Harleston stared at her dumbly. The young lady before him was a far cry from the aged nurse or valet he had vaguely expected to open the door. She was beautiful.

She was tall and slender, with shoulders and neck so graceful that an artist might have painted them with one fluid stroke. Her dark, almost black hair was tied softly back in a chignon, but even in that poor light it shone with a rich lustre. Her features were fine and delicate and her eyes, too dark to call brown, were large and expressive. Right now, they regarded him with a mixture of reserve, curiosity and suspicion.

Realizing that he had been standing in a most improper silence while staring in the rudest fashion, Lord Harleston recalled himself to his errand and made his introduction. "I have come to call on your father at his request," he finished, trying to remove the trace of concern he detected.

Her brow puckered slightly. "At his request?" she asked. "I do not recall having written to you for my father, my lord."

Lord Harleston smiled. He liked the smooth, even tone of her voice with its gently questioning lilt. "The letter was written by Monsieur Renard, Miss Johnstone." Surprise lit her eyes but she was still clearly perplexed. "Perhaps your father thought it would be more proper to contact me through another gentleman," he said, dismissing the letter lightly. For whatever reason the captain had need of him, it was obvious that his daughter knew nothing of the matter.

"Perhaps," she said, flushing. The soft rosy colour spread slowly through her pale skin, tinging it pleasantly. "Please come in, Lord Harleston," she said suddenly, "and forgive me for keeping you in the corridor. I could not be certain . . ." She did not finish her sentence, but the baron could guess her fears on her father's behalf.

He stepped forward into the room, but unable to take his eyes off her face, he once again forgot to duck and brought his head sharply up against the top of the doorway.

"Ow!" he cried involuntarily as the spot he had hit before suffered its second blow.

"My lord!" exclaimed Miss Johnstone in extreme distress. "I am so very sorry! Please, oh, please, sit down and let me look at your head." He lowered himself into a chair and allowed her to examine the lump. She was hovering near him with an expression of great pity which he found, under the circumstances, particularly pleasing. The initial pain of the encounter had already passed, but he permitted himself the luxury of sitting to have his head bathed with a cool cloth.

"Oh, you poor man! Does it hurt dreadfully?"

Lord Harleston uttered a groan, despite the fact that her distress was totally out of proportion to the discomfort he was feeling.

Miss Johnstone continued to make comforting sounds and sponged the afflicted spot with such gentle effectiveness that after a while Lord Harleston had to smile at his fraudulent behaviour. She had a sweet, natural essence which seemed to act like a tonic on him and he felt even better than he had before his head had been bumped.

"You will think me the greatest coward, Miss Johnstone," he said eventually, remembering that Monsieur Renard had urged him to hurry to the captain. "But that is not at all the case. We military men are tough as nails, you know. It is merely a surface wound, and if I had not just bumped the same spot out in the street, I should have taken the blow like a man."

She laughed but, pitying him even further, put her hand to her mouth and regarded him with sympathetic anguish.

"I am afraid these old buildings were not designed for someone like me."

"No," she agreed, taking in his large frame with a shy smile. "Frenchmen, as a rule, are not so... tall." Suddenly self-conscious, she withdrew her hand from his head. "If you are quite recovered now, perhaps I should tell my father you are here."

"By all means."

Lord Harleston followed her with his eyes until she disappeared and then gazed about him at the room where she had left him. It was a small, sparsely furnished parlour with only the one chair in which he now sat. Before the door closed behind Miss Johnstone, he had caught a glimpse of the foot of a bed and another chair upon which rested a basket of needlework and he deduced that Miss Johnstone was in the habit of sitting beside her father's bed, keeping her hands occupied while waiting to be needed. The parlour must hardly be used.

What the deuce had made the captain drag his daughter into this unpleasant business? he wondered. Until this evening he had not known of her existence. But that did not surprise him, for his friendship with Captain Johnstone, although always of the best, had been purely professional. He could not imagine the old beau spending much time at home. The family hearth was no place for him. He pictured Miss Johnstone's graceful figure as she had swept from the room and a sudden flash of irritation seized him. What a dreary life the captain had brought her to!

The door to the bedroom opened again, and Miss Johnstone beckoned to him to enter. She was smiling again, although still with a touch of curiosity. "He seems delighted you've come," she said as he entered. "I think your visit will do him good."

Lord Harleston took a step toward the bed and heard her departing footsteps behind him. The room, he could see, although simple, was clean and comfortable. A lamp on a table threw a light on the wan, lined face on the bed pillows and it came as a shock, even to a man inured to the sight of his companions' dying, to see the change that had been effected in the four years since he had seen Captain Johnstone. Even in his illness, though, there was a spotless air about him and the cuffs of his nightshirt were trimmed with lace. In a moment, a pale hand waved him over and a familiar twinkle lit the faded eyes.

"So it's Harleston, now, is it?" teased the gruff voice. "You've come into your inheritance since I saw you. And not sold out?"

"No, sir," he said, grasping the captain's hand firmly. "I thought I should see it to the end. But I suppose I shall have to go home soon and face my responsibilities."

"Good lad! I thought you would last. Never feared you wouldn't make it, either, in spite of your madcap ways. You're too big to fall." He seemed to gather strength from the young hand in his. "I never would have sold out, either, you know, if that scoundrel Battington hadn't won my last sous at faro." The recollection did not seem to trouble him much.

"Tell me what I can do for you," Lord Harleston said gently, but the older man waved it aside.

"Not yet. That can wait. Tell me what is going on in Paris." His tired eyes lit with eagerness.

Lord Harleston grinned. He had not forgotten his captain's appetite for gossip, nor his dandyish ways. Pulling a chair close to the bed, he sat and began to relate the on-dits he knew would appeal most to the old gentleman.

"Bacon and Arnold of the 10th and Sir Charles Smith have introduced four-in-hand teams to Paris," he said after bringing the captain up to date on their old corps. "They meet near the Café de Paris and drive to the Boulevard Beaumarchais, and then back the new archway they are building, the Arc de ꞏphe. They seem to be drawing quite a crowd. Of course, Sir Charles takes up one or two beauties to ride beside him," he added.

"The idiots!" said Captain Johnstone, laughing and then lapsing into a cough. The paroxysm lasted an alarmingly long time before it subsided, and when it did he spoke in a weaker voice. "Won't be happy, I suppose, until they've broken their necks."

"They've got up a bit of horse racing, too. It's somewhat better than the French races, which look like a contest between the Gendarmes and the National Guard. The mounted police follow so closely after the horses that sometimes they finish before them." Lord Harleston was rewarded with another chuckle.

"What are they wearing?"

"The fashions are not at all what one sees in London. The men's coats are invariably blue or black and strangely made. They hang down to the ankles and are baggily cut."

The old man's eyebrows rose with a suggestion of distaste. "And the ladies?"

"Scanty skirts, quite short, with little or no waist. Enormous, unattractive bonnets which protrude a distance from the face—and fans.

"I went to a soirée the other evening in the Rue de Clichy—Lady Oxford's. You would scarcely believe the number of English in Paris now, and half of them, it seemed, were at her *hôtel*." He went on to list some of the guests. "And they are all, at least the men, frequenting the Salon des Etrangers and the Palais Royal."

The pale hand grasped his again eagerly. "Tell me about the Palais Royal."

Lord Harleston suppressed a smile. "All right. The houses—and there are a vast number of them—are all pretty much the same. The ground floor of one, I remember, was occupied by a jeweller, and his stock consisted of the finest gems I've ever seen. Diamonds and rubies of almost unbelievable size. Then, upstairs, on the first floor, were the gaming tables."

"What do they play?"

"Mostly rouge et noir and roulette. You find every class of person around them, from the King of Prussia to the workman throwing away his last sous. The tables are usually separated by class, of course, but there is something for everyone." He spoke quietly and without enthusiasm, not liking the feverish look in the older man's eyes. "And up above that are the ladies."

Some of the glaze disappeared from the captain's stare, and he lifted his eyebrows at his young friend. "Want to tell me about the ladies?" he asked.

Lord Harleston laughed. "I'd better not, sir. But I will tell you that they live in a style of splendour that has much to do with the activities below."

Captain Johnstone nodded. He seemed more weary suddenly. Lord Harleston watched him for a while without speaking, wondering what regrets, if any, were passing through the older man's head. After a moment, the captain patted his hand weakly and looked at him soberly.

"You must be wondering why I wrote to you," he began, watching for the baron's reaction with some concern. The young peer returned his grasp firmly.

"I am ready to do whatever it is you need of me," was the simple answer.

Captain Johnstone stared at him a moment more, but seemed reassured. Finally he spoke, "It is Susan."

"Miss Johnstone?" said Lord Harleston. Since seeing the captain's daughter, he had privately come to the conclusion that she must be the subject of the letter he had received. But Miss Johnstone was already of an age (he guessed her to be about twenty-five) that she could not be made his responsibility. And the baron suspected that she had not been told of the letter because she would not have sent it had she known its purpose. He spoke hesitantly, "Monsieur Renard mentioned there was nothing left . . ."

The captain nodded, "Did he tell you the bailiff nabbed me?"

Lord Harleston's brow clouded. "You went to prison?" The thought distressed him.

"Yes. I signed up to be a member of the Fleet." Captain Johnstone's eyes twinkled again as he repeated the old joke. "Three months on board for a bit of whitewashing. Water under the bridge."

"And you came here afterward?"

The old man shook his head slowly and a glimmer of pride lit his eyes. Then he said, "Susan sprang me."

Lord Harleston started. "She what?"

The captain's eyes danced. "She smuggled me out. Took me out on a white pony and made straight for the coast. Had a ship all ready and waiting, and we were on the high seas before I could blink an eye. She must have been saving every penny I'd sent her to pull it off." He chuckled.

"Did she, by God!" Lord Harleston was still stunned. He was having trouble reconciling such a desperate deed with the graceful, almost fragile creature he had seen in the parlour. He looked back at the door, almost expecting to see her there in a different disguise.

Captain Johnstone seemed to divine his thoughts. "Aye, she's a beauty like her mother. But I guess there's a bit of the old man in her, too." He eyed his visitor with satisfaction as a hint of colour tinged Lord Harleston's face. "You see the problem now, don't you?" he continued. "She's in trouble with the authorities, and there's no hope of her going back to England when I'm dead."

"But surely she knew that would be the case?" said Lord Harleston, speaking as much to himself as to the captain. He was wondering what had possessed her to do such a rash thing when her father's sentence would have passed in only three months.

"Yes," Captain Johnstone admitted, raising his eyebrows expressively, "but you don't know Susan. I wrote to her, you see, when they caught up with me, just so she would know why I wasn't sending her any money. I've tried to send her some whenever I had it.

She's been living with an old governess of hers." An intimation of guilt crossed his face. "Anyway, I hadn't expected her to post straight down to see me. And the deuce of it was I had just taken ill." He stopped his narrative with an air of having concluded.

Lord Harleston waited expectantly for a moment before asking, "But why did she plan your escape?"

Captain Johnstone looked at him in surprise and then, remembering, suddenly grinned. "I forget you do not know her yet," he said. Then he explained. "Susan is not what you'd call bold—she doesn't put herself forward. But show her some poor unfortunate beggar and she'll raise the Lord Mayor if it'll do him any good. One look at me in that place was enough. She had plans to get me out of there by nightfall, and by the end of the week it was done." He eyed his visitor hopefully as a look of admiration came over Lord Harleston's face.

The young man was lost in thought. An occasional smile wavered about his lips. In a while, though, he seemed to recall his present circumstances and faced the captain with eager determination.

"What is it you wish me to do?" he asked.

"Get her back into England" was the quick answer. Captain Johnstone was not discouraged by the answering spark in the baron's brown eyes. "She can go back to her old governess and be perfectly safe there. If the authorities don't know she's back, they won't try to look for her. And I'm certain the whole thing will blow over eventually."

He waited. With any other man he would have expected questions and protests, demands as to how the thing was to be done. But not with Harleston. Captain Johnstone could see the wheels turning inside the young man's head as he thought out his plan of action, and he was heartened by the enthusiasm in his expression. Harleston always did like a tight spot.

In a minute, the baron turned to him and held out his hand again. "Done," he said.

The old man grasped at it gratefully. Words of thanks did not come easily. "I should have been better to her, you see," he said instead. "A pretty girl like Susan—she should have had parties, balls, more fine dresses. And now," he ended weakly, "with no dowry..." Lord Harleston pressed the hand in his but did not speak. There was nothing to be said, for what the captain said was true.

The old man's clasp grew weaker. "I always hoped the next hand would be a winner," he explained almost petulantly now. "Some of them were such near things." His mind drifted as he replayed those old hands in his mind. Lord Harleston gave him a gentle pat on the shoulder.

"You needn't worry about your daughter," he said to ease the captain's thoughts. It was too late for guilt. "I shall see she gets back to England safely, and I'll be happy to do what I can to secure her future."

The captain came back to the present with a start. "One more thing," he said in an urgent tone. "You mustn't breathe a word of this to Susan. If she catches on to it, she'll be gone before you can get back. Just tell Renard to send you word when I'm gone. He'll manage to keep her here for a while—knows all about it." His speech was cut off by the sound of the door opening.

Lord Harleston turned to see Susan enter the room and rose to his feet. She smiled hesitantly at him and moved gracefully toward the bed. He watched her with barely concealed admiration.

"I know you have enjoyed your visit, Papa, but I think it has been long enough for now." Captain Johnstone looked once more at the baron for reassurance.

Lord Harleston turned to address him, glancing now and then back at his daughter as though drawn in some invisible way. "I will leave you to your rest now, sir," he said. "Urgent business takes me back to Paris," he added with a wink for the captain's benefit. "But I shall give myself the pleasure of returning soon." The old man seemed too tired to answer, but as he lifted a hand in farewell, his smile was peaceful. The two young people went out and closed the door.

SHUTTERING HIS EYES to welcome sleep, the captain recalled Lord Harleston's expression as he had gazed at Susan's face. He chuckled softly to himself. No, he had not been wrong when he had written to Harleston. The young devil would have her back in England in a trice and settled comfortably as before.

A twinge of guilt disturbed him momentarily but was banished. He had done what he could to deliver her into good hands.

CHAPTER TWO

THREE WEEKS LATER, Susan was sitting in the parlour putting the final stitches in her mourning. She was already dressed in black. Her father had lived slightly longer than expected, and she reflected gladly that he had seemed calmer the last few weeks. Ever since Lord Harleston's visit, she recalled. She wondered what the purpose of that visit had been, but all her father had said on the subject was that he had a yearning to see his old favourite before he died. Somehow Susan did not quite believe it. She still did not understand why Monsieur Renard had written the letter, and she remembered her surprise upon answering the baron's knock and finding such a handsome young man at the door.

Her needle paused for a moment. Surely Lord Harleston's hair was the blondest she had ever seen except on a small child. But where one might have expected to find blue eyes, his had been a golden brown, and she suspected the sun would turn his smooth skin to a becoming bronze. Susan shook herself and took up her needle once again. Whatever could have turned her thoughts so strangely? she wondered.

She tried to interest herself in her work, but put it down in another few minutes with a sigh. She really must confront Monsieur Renard today. The captain's funeral had been four days ago and it was time for her to be leaving. She could not impose on her father's old friend any longer. Monsieur Renard spoke often of an old debt, but that debt was to her father and had been amply repaid.

Susan had had many talks with the bookseller about her future plans and he had promised to help her find a situation as a governess or an English mistress in a school, but so far he had not done so. When she had last spoken of it to him he had told her that he was almost certain of a position not far from Calais if she would only wait a few more days. But his delay caused her to worry that something had happened to cancel that prospect. She would have to talk to him about going to an agency tomorrow.

A knock at the door took her by surprise, but she hoped that Monsieur Renard had come at last with news of employment. Opening it, however, she was amazed to see her father's friend Lord Harleston again.

His large frame loomed in the narrow hallway as it had on the night of his first visit. The thought struck her that he was not so much big as tall and powerful with broad shoulders over narrow hips. He had swept off his beaver and the light of day gleamed on his fair hair.

"Miss Johnstone?" he began. He smiled at her in such a way that she knew he had received word of her father's death.

"Lord Harleston—please come in," she said, backing slightly into the room. But as she moved she recalled his entry on the previous visit and quickly put up a warning hand. Smiling his thanks, but with a sheepish look, Lord Harleston ducked and missed hitting his head a third time.

"I'm afraid you are come too late to call on my father again," she said evenly and without emotion. He noted it with approval. The black of her dress did nothing to diminish the dark gleam in her hair and eyes and, despite its sad purpose, became her well.

"I know," he answered, "I had heard. May I offer my condolences?" She nodded and he continued. "My business, however, is with you, Miss Johnstone. If I might have a word…" Susan gave a curious smile and indicated a chair, which he took before speaking again.

"I have come," Lord Harleston began, watching carefully for her reaction and treading cautiously as he went on, "in answer to your father's dying request." Susan's eyes opened in surprise, but she listened as he explained his reason for calling. In a very short while, those eyes were flashing their refusal.

"No," she said simply, rising to her feet and facing the baron. He could see that she was not angry, but rather distressed to think herself a burden. "That is absolutely absurd! I see no reason why you should be involved in my ridiculous predicament." Lord Harleston suppressed a smile. This was much the reaction he had anticipated and for which he was prepared.

He allowed a wounded look to cross his features. "But Miss Johnstone, you must understand. This puts me in a very uncomfortable position. To be denying your father's last request of me... A man who once saved my life... Why, it's unthinkable!"

Susan, clearly struck by the awkwardness of his situation, became more distressed than ever. "I am so sorry, Lord Harleston, but surely you must see. I cannot let you become involved. It would be quite wrong of me!"

His hurt look stiffened slightly. "I see. I should be interfering in your plans. You have other friends, perhaps—others who are more trusted, with whom you are more intimate...?"

"Oh, no!" she said quickly, hoping to soothe his wounded feelings. "There is no one else. That is, Monsieur Renard is doing what he can to find me a position in a school or a household, but there is no one else I had rather turn to." She blushed confusedly. "Surely you can understand."

"That you had rather stay in France amongst strangers than return to your home?" he asked gently.

Susan's eyes met his and then fell, overcome by the sudden sympathy. "No," she answered quietly. His kindness demanded honesty. "If I could have what I truly wish, it would be to return to my old governess, Miss Irons. She runs a school now and I could help her with her pupils. And we are good companions. But there is no way for me to go back, Lord Harleston," she said calmly, raising her eyes again in a determined fashion.

Feeling, nevertheless, that he was beginning to break down her resistance, the baron allowed his enthusiasm to creep into his voice. "No way? Surely not, Miss Johnstone. Why, how can you say that—you—when you acted with such courage on your father's behalf?"

Susan flushed uncomfortably. "Did he tell you that? But that was different," she protested. "It was necessary. I could not leave Papa in the Fleet Prison to die in discomfort."

"Of course you couldn't," Lord Harleston agreed. "He was your father."

Susan looked even more ill at ease. "It was not *that* precisely," she said. Then, in answer to his puzzled expression, she explained, "My father and I had never been close, you see. In the past many years, I had scarcely seen him. It was just that he looked so old, and sick, and pitiful...in that dreary place...." She allowed her voice to trail off, looking to him for understanding.

"Naturally," he said, hoping that his fascination with her unreasoning heart was not evident in his expression. If fleeing the country with a fugitive was a reasonable action to her, then getting her back into England by a slightly unorthodox method should not be so unacceptable. "But you must have disguised yourself somehow to have dealt with the smugglers? How was it done? A mask? Or veils?''

To his surprise, Susan's skin turned a rosy pink and her voice dropped to a near whisper. "Not exactly," she said, and then reluctantly admitted, "I wore men's clothes.''

Harleston's mouth fell open, but then tactfully snapped shut. "Admirable!" he said, struggling to keep a straight face. "Much the best plan! You were much safer that way amongst such a desperate gang. Well, then, you see, what could be simpler than to do it again? I should accompany you this time, however," he said as he saw her bristle.

"I'm afraid not, Lord Harleston," she answered crisply. "Despite my clearly outrageous behaviour on that occasion, I take no particular pleasure from such masquerades. And I absolutely refuse to participate in another.''

"Oh, naturally," he said again. "I mean, of course, it would be distasteful to you." He felt slightly disappointed, but then brightening, said, "But fortunately, I have my own plan which is much simpler and much more conventional. Let me explain it to you." Susan was still looking ruffled, but she did not refuse to listen, so he went on.

"Do you speak French?''

She frowned anxiously. "Yes, but not particularly well.''

"But enough to get around about town?''

"Yes.''

"Good. That will be sufficient." He threw her a measuring look before continuing. "What I propose is for you to assume the identity of a Frenchwoman, a widow. But of an Englishman, you see. You will be returning to your husband's estates in England. Your widow's status will allow you to arrange things more to your satisfaction and will give you reason to wear a veil."

"But..."

"I can arrange for all the papers you will need to enter England. It will be a matter of days."

Susan hesitated before posing any more arguments. "But won't it appear strange, even so, for me to be travelling alone?"

"Oh, you will not be alone," he assured her. "I have plans for your retinue. And there will be no trouble," he added, watching her anxiously as a look of suspicion crossed her face.

Yet something about his innocent expression seemed to tickle her, for she finally laughed. "All right, my lord. And of whom shall this retinue consist?"

"Well," he said, "first of all—and this is quite a bit of luck, really—there will be your personal maid. You see, I have had my man ask about and he has found a young person, an English girl, who was discharged recently by her employers. She has been stranded here ever since and cannot return to England unless someone engages her for the return."

"Oh, the poor girl!" cried Susan. Her own problems were forgotten at the thought of the wretch's difficulty. "By all means, we must assist her!" Her brow furrowed in absorbed concern.

Lord Harleston suppressed a gleeful chuckle. Captain Johnstone had given him the perfect key to winning his daughter's agreement. "Yes," he agreed earnestly. "I feel it to be imperative, too. And, of course, you will need a groom, as well."

"A groom?" she asked vaguely, still deep in thought about the poor serving maid.

"Yes, for your carriage. I have made arrangements for one to be there when we get to Dover. We must get the girl—Peg, I believe her name is—to London before we discharge her again." This he added as she looked at him anxiously.

"Of course," Susan agreed. "It would be cruel to discharge her before she gets as far as London to speak to an agency. But who is this groom? And did you say we?"

Lord Harleston took a deep breath. "Yes, I did," he admitted. "You see, I shall be the groom."

Susan's eyes widened in horror, but before she could protest, he added in firm tones, "I'm afraid I must insist upon it, Miss Johnstone. You see, it was your father's last request, and I could not reconcile it with my conscience to create a potentially hazardous situation for you and then not see it through. I must insist, I repeat, on being there with you, and obviously I cannot travel as myself under the circumstances."

"But as a groom . . . !"

"There will be no difficulty. In fact, I think I shall enjoy it. Unlike you, I rather like this sort of masquerade. And remember, travelling as myself I would be likely to call undesirable attention to you. What possible reason could a peer have for travelling with an unattached lady that would not excite curiosity? But your groom—what could be more normal?"

Susan opened her mouth to protest, but shut it again. The plan was outrageous, but Lord Harleston appeared to be quite eager to place himself in jeopardy. And then there was the maid. The girl must be got home to England, and she herself had no money to give her. Looking up at Lord Harleston, she noted his firm expression and reflected that he would probably refuse to help the girl without her compliance. But suddenly something else occurred to her which loomed larger than all her other objections.

Susan folded her hands serenely before her and spoke in a calm but final voice.

"I am very much obliged to you, Lord Harleston, for offering to take these risks on my behalf, and I confess, the thought of returning to England was so tempting as to make me consider your rash proposal. But I have no money, and I will not accept any further charity."

She looked at him. In spite of the delicacy of her features, there was a firmness about her which almost took him aback. An impartial observer watching these two at that moment might have said there was no way to tell which would come out the winner. But Lord Harleston had not come to this campaign with the intention of losing and he reentered the battle with barely a moment's hesitation.

"If that is your only objection, Miss Johnstone," he said with an assumption of grave sincerity, "then I must consider the point resolved. Your father entrusted me with a small sum to accomplish your safe return. I should have mentioned it earlier, but I did not regard it as a material consideration." Waiting for her response, he did not allow his glance to waver.

Susan stared back at him incredulously, but the steadiness of his expression at last had its effect.

"How much?" she asked suddenly.

"Fifty pounds." She opened her mouth again to question him, but he continued. "He kept it concealed upon his person with the intention of having it sent to you upon his death. Then, when you brought him here, he decided it should be used to return you safely to your governess."

Susan was frowning with confusion. "But Monsieur Renard . . . We are so much in his debt. . . ."

Lord Harleston shook his head. "No. This was your father's wish. The knowledge that his own excesses were responsible for your not being better established weighed on him heavily at the end."

Susan blushed, but her smile was quite tender. "I did not know he thought of my welfare at all," she admitted shyly.

Right then and there, Lord Harleston vowed that never, even if they submitted him to the rack, would he ever divulge that he had invented the said fifty pounds. He watched her for a moment more, noting with a peculiar elation the softness of her black lashes against her pale cheeks. Then he stood up and began to pace briskly about the room as he spoke.

"Good. Now that we have that settled, we can plan our voyage. Have you a black veil to use along with your mourning?"

Susan started at the brisk turn of the conversation, but answered automatically, "Yes."

"Excellent! What I propose, as I said before, is that you assume the role of a Frenchwoman, widow of an Englishman. I have already set the plan in motion and will have your papers for you as soon as we decide upon a name."

"A name?" Susan had been thinking, fondly and regretfully, about her scapegrace father, and was not keeping up with Lord Harleston's rapid planning.

He smiled. "Yes. You must have a name. Something English, of course. Your first name, if anyone should ask, may remain Susan, although you must remember to say it the French way—Suzanne."

"Yes, of course."

He was facing her now and his voice had taken on a note of eagerness. "Is there a surname you've always fancied, something you would remember to answer to if called?"

"No, not that I think of." Her mind had suddenly gone blank.

"Well, then, let's see. The best way to go about choosing a name would be to pick a location—from the map. Have you got one?"

"Yes," she answered quickly and stepped to a small escritoire. She was happy to be able to provide something instead of standing about like a dazed fool. "I do have a map of England. I used it to guide the coachman to the coast," she explained as she produced it.

"Wonderful! Now, let's see." He opened the map and allowed his eyes to roam over it. "What a lot to choose from! Well, I suppose anything will do. I'll just point to a spot at random and see what it says." Susan suppressed a smile as Lord Harleston, abandoning all his dignity as a peer, closed his eyes tightly as though fearing to cheat and jabbed a finger at the map. He opened them and looked closely at the spot beside his finger.

"Barton-upon-Humber," he read carefully.

Beside him, Susan giggled, and he looked up with an answering grin. "Not very likely, is it?" he admitted.

"I can see how it might lead to all sorts of uncomfortable questions," Susan agreed. "Besides, I don't think I could pronounce it with a French accent."

"No! By Jove! I suppose not. Then, I shan't suggest Stow-on-the-Wold or Newcastle-on-Trent, either.

Let's give it another try, shall we?" He closed his eyes again and this time Susan smiled broadly.

"Husbands Bosworth," he read when his finger had fallen again. Susan hooted with laughter and covered her mouth with her hand in an attempt to smother it.

"I suppose," she volunteered, "that my lamented spouse's name was *Mr.* Husbands Bosworth." Lord Harleston laughed.

"Now look here," he said finally, struggling for a note of reason. "Why not just drop the Husbands part and be Mrs. Bosworth? It's a perfectly good name."

Susan shook her head with comic regret. "No, I'm sorry. It is too late. I shouldn't be able to think of Bosworth without giggling now, and if you happened to call me Mrs. Bosworth, pulling a forelock or something, and looked at me as you are doing now, I should just dissolve." She could not keep herself from smiling, and Lord Harleston thought privately how much laughter became her lovely face.

"I see. Yes. That's a reasonable objection," he agreed. "I am glad to see that I shall be in the employ of someone with her wits about her. Well, perhaps the random method is not the best." He turned back to the map. "Let's just look at the next town along the way. Hmmm...Market Harborough. Not very likely, I suppose." He glanced up with a comical expression of defeat. "I really thought this would be a good method."

Susan took pity on him and moved closer to his side. "Here," she said. "Let me see what there is.

Perhaps I'll see something I like." She leaned over the map and dragged her finger gently across it.

"Chapel-en-le-Frith," she murmured. "Much Wenlock." She declined to meet his eye. "Amazing, isn't it, how many are completely unsuitable. Ashby-de-la-Zouch." She smiled again. "Perhaps another direction would be better."

Lord Harleston watched her as she frowned thoughtfully over the map. The smooth curve of her brow wrinkled only slightly and then lifted as she hit upon another humorous name. Slight wisps of her lustrous hair had escaped their pins and were curling provocatively around her tiny ears. He wondered how she would react if she suddenly raised her head and noticed how close they were standing, and how closely he had been watching her. Suddenly, however, her finger stopped and her eyes opened wider with interest as she silently mouthed some word.

"What is it?" he asked, arrested by her expression.

"Faringdon," she said. She straightened and looked at him with an expression of triumph. "I shall be Mrs. Faringdon. It is a perfectly sensible name and I know I shall remember it because I have been there."

"Good girl!" said the baron, pretending not to notice her sudden blush as she became aware of his nearness. "I am glad that one of us has been able to put my brilliant plan to good use. And now," he said, sitting down again as Susan moved back to her chair. "A little rehearsal." He told her of the plans he had made for his valet and former batman to engage Peg, the maid, and send her along to Susan for approval.

"So all you will have to do is pose a few questions, just to make her think you have taken the proper steps, and send her away with plans to come back the morning we leave for Dover. I will send word the second I'm back with the papers and meet you both at the quay."

"But isn't Peg to be let in on the plan?" asked Susan. "I should not like to have to keep up the deception under my own roof."

Lord Harleston shook his head. "I do not think we had better tell her. It is possible she would give everything away." Susan lifted an eyebrow questioningly. Lord Harleston, with a hint of sheepishness, explained, "I understand she was turned off for incompetence." Susan raised her brow even further. "And insolence," he added reluctantly.

Both her eyes were wide open now and regarding him with reproach, but she said nothing.

"It will only be for one day," he reminded her. "We shall press on to London directly upon reaching Dover. And if she becomes curious, you may just demand silence. And, of course, your English will not be the best, so she will think you quite foreign and beyond understanding anyway."

Susan looked slightly ruffled and anxious. "I am not a play-actress, Lord Harleston," she reminded him.

He laughed. "No, but acting is fun! Come now, let's practise." He addressed a few questions to her in fluid French and she responded shyly but competently. "There. That's quite good. But you must not be timid. In fact, the more you assert yourself the better you will be believed. The only ticklish spot that I can foresee will be talking to the customs officials. They can get rather nasty. But if they do, you must simply throw a tantrum. Call them something demeaning! Let me hear you say, 'Non, non, non! Imbécile!'"

"Non, non, non, imbécile."

"With more anger! And building toward the last non. Non, non, non! Imbécile!"

Susan complied with greater vigour and then suppressed a laugh as Lord Harleston rewarded her with an enthusiastic, "Excellent!"

"But what if I start to laugh?" she asked.

"Nonsense," he said simply. "If we must resort to an outburst, you will not feel like laughing. And I shall be there to punish you if you do," he cautioned her with a stern look.

In spite of herself, Susan dimpled as though she would like nothing better. But to cover up this improper reaction, she quickly pointed out, "And what about you, Lord Harleston? Perhaps you should rehearse your part—I presume you have never played a groom before?" She threw him a glance as if to say that really nothing would surprise her less.

"No, I haven't," he retorted in like spirit.

"Well, you shall have to dress the part."

He nodded and made a gesture of dismissal, as though the detail were merely a trifle. "My man shall get clothes for me."

She looked him over critically. Their shared mirth had overcome her shyness and now a feeling of impish elation bubbled up inside her. "You certainly cannot wear your hair like that," she said. "It must be cut unevenly and tousled. You might even put a few pieces of hay in it," she added facetiously, "for verisimilitude—as it were."

"As it were, indeed," agreed Lord Harleston with an appreciative grin. "I am glad to see that you are entering into the spirit of the adventure, Miss Johnstone. And I must say I am looking forward to it with increasing delight."

Susan felt herself blushing furiously, but could do nothing to stop it. "As to your manner," she said rather quickly to hide her confusion, "you might adopt a rather bovine expression. And I suppose it might do to cultivate a suitably illiterate sound, like . . . *ur*."

Lord Harleston strove to keep his lips from twitching as he stared at her ominously, but she ignored his threats. "And there is one more thing, my lord," she mentioned hesitantly. He gazed at her with a curious smile and strangely, she could not meet his eye. "What must I call you?"

"Call me?" He seemed distracted.

"Yes. I cannot very well call my groom 'Lord Harleston,'" she said reasonably, recovering her composure as he seemed to lose his.

His eyes lit with understanding. "Oh, of course, I see what you mean. No. I cannot remain Lord Harleston. My name must be something like Jem or Ned . . . Wait," he said as an idea came to him, "what about Tom?" He watched her closely for a reaction.

"Tom," she said looking him over as if trying the name on for size. "Yes, Tom would be good. It suits you."

His expression flickered for a brief moment, as if some private joke had occurred to him. But he gave no explanation beyond saying, "Good. I have always fancied the name Tom. It has such a steady, reliable ring to it. A good English-sounding sort of name," he expounded. "It calls to mind hard work and fair play and all the proper values."

Susan eyed him with misgiving, so he stopped where he was. "Well, then, Miss Johnstone," he said, rising and picking up his hat. "If there are no other matters we need to discuss, I shall go back to Paris for those papers. For Mrs. Faringdon," he recalled, raising his first finger.

Susan rose with him. "Lord Harleston, before you go . . ." she began in a more serious tone.

"Tom," he reminded her.

"Yes, of course." She coloured. "Lord—"

"Tom!"

Susan eyed him stubbornly. "Lord *Tom*, then. You must let me thank you sincerely for all you are doing on my behalf."

Lord Harleston smiled reassuringly. "Believe me...Mrs. Faringdon," he interjected impishly. "It will be the greatest pleasure. I am looking forward to the adventure with delightful anticipation."

"But..." began Susan. She misliked his flippant attitude and felt he must be cautioned again of the risks. And be given a chance to change his mind.

"Please do not worry," he said more seriously. She looked deeply into his eyes and suddenly saw something she had not seen before. It was some elusive quality, too complex to define, but it came of a mixture of bravery, intelligence and wisdom. This must be what his soldiers recognize in him, she realized. But, she added to herself wryly, it was no wonder she had not seen it at once in a man who bumped his head twice the first time he came to call.

"All right," she agreed, feeling strangely comforted. "But thank you, Lord..." He held up one finger. "*Lord Tom*," she called after him as he went out the door.

CHAPTER THREE

SIX DAYS LATER, heavily veiled in black crepe, Susan smiled with relief at the welcome sight of Tom's figure awaiting her on the quay. With Peg at her side, she wove her way through the crowd waiting to embark until she reached the spot where he was standing. But, she reflected, if she had not seen the sun's gleam upon his newly tousled hair, she might not have recognised him so quickly in his present garb.

He was dressed in serviceable breeches and a plain cotton shirt which, she could see under the homespun woolen cloak he also wore, was open in front to reveal the musculature of his strong neck. There were no pieces of straw arranged artfully as she had suggested, but his hair had been roughly cut and tousled, which, curiously, became him even more than his carefully arranged and pomaded locks. Now she could see that his hair was naturally straight and fine, and that it shone in streaks wherever the light touched its white-gold strands. Tom was bowing to her with the humblest servility and pulling his forelock, and she was grateful for the veil which concealed her smiling response to the gleam in his brown-gold eyes.

Suddenly there was a gasp beside her and she turned to find Peg gazing at Tom with unconcealed admiration. *"Coo,"* she said in a drawn-out undertone. Lord Harleston looked up startled at first, and then, blushing, glanced back quickly at his false employer.

Susan's first reaction was one of pure amusement. The dismay on Lord Harleston's face was so comical (it practically begged her assistance,) that she could hardly refrain from laughing. But as Peg moved closer to him and struck a flirtatious pose, something inside Susan instinctively revolted.

"Peg!" she said with sharp authority. "See to my bags at once! We shall be boarding shortly." The girl mumbled a graceless "Yes, miss," and moved reluctantly toward the street where the hired fiacre was waiting with the baggage. Her eyes strayed back toward Tom from time to time until the crowd concealed him from her view entirely.

"Phew!" said Tom, turning to face Susan with an expression of relief. He spoke softly so as not to be overheard by the other passengers. "Is that the maid I've saddled you with? My apologies! Do you think she'll do as far as London?"

"Oh, yes," said Susan. "Certainly that far." But her voice betrayed her misgivings. As she looked at Tom, she could hardly blame Peg for her instant attraction to him, for his physique alone was enough to charm female eyes. And together with his blond hair... Susan shook herself mentally, thinking that she was hardly better than the maid herself. Then she frowned, remembering her first and only encounter with Peg until this morning.

It had gone far differently from her expectations.

Within minutes of admitting her to Monsieur Renard's parlour, Susan had begun to eye the young girl standing before her with increasing unease. Peg was a comely maid with blondish hair and a clear complexion, save for a few small freckles on the top of her nose which did not at all detract from her appearance. Moreover, her figure, which she made no attempt to conceal, was blessed with curves any man would have found alluring.

It was not her obvious charms which distressed Susan, however, though she did wish the girl would button her blouse a bit closer to the neck and debated whether, as her employer, she might not suggest it to her. It was her *manner* which Susan found disconcerting.

She had greeted the girl with a warmth not usually extended to creatures applying for a domestic position, but which reflected Susan's own pity for the girl's situation. However, Peg's answering tirade about unfair employers in general and her latest in particular had done nothing to increase Susan's confidence in her own position. For the past many years, the captain had not provided enough money for his daughter to enjoy the luxury of a personal maid, so dealing with servants, uppity or otherwise, was not a matter of habit.

And now she was finding that, far from the gratitude she might have expected for saving the girl from an awkward situation, and farther still from the loyalty, even devotion, that she had allowed her tender heart to envisage, she was confronted with brash arrogance and patent dislike. It was most disillusioning.

She had posed Peg the minimum number of innocuous questions she felt necessary to allay the girl's suspicions that her prospective employer might not be all that she seemed. Peg's answers had not been very satisfactory, however, and Susan reflected that no honest person would have engaged her, based upon them, for Peg had scarcely any skills, training or experience. Nevertheless, Susan had engaged her and had explained what was required of her until they left for England.

"But can't I stay 'ere?" Peg protested in a whiny voice which implied the great cruelty she was suffering.

"*Non!* You may not," said Susan sternly. She was finding that the girl brought out a severity in her that was as genuine in this case as it was rare in others. The effort of speaking with a fake foreign accent was already taking its toll upon her and Peg's argumentative disposition called for lengthy explanations. Remembering Lord Harleston's tutoring, she decided not to give one on this occasion, but to retreat behind a haughty facade.

"'Ere," she said, giving the girl three silver francs from the money Lord Harleston had sent her. "Zat will be enough to maintain you in adequate lodgings until I call for you. If for any reason our voyage is delayed, you may come to me for more, but I expect to send word in two or s'ree days."

"Yes, miss," agreed Peg reluctantly, but obviously mollified by the feel of silver in her hand.

"You must call me *madame*, Peg," Susan corrected her.

"Oll right, madam," said Peg with a scornful glance, "but you don't have no ring."

Susan glanced quickly down at her hand as the truth of Peg's accusation sank in. Drat the girl! But neither she nor Lord Harleston had thought about a ring, and if Peg, ignorant as she was, should think it strange for her not to have one, what might the customs officials think?

Susan drew herself up and gave Peg her haughtiest look. "It is at ze jeweller's being repaired. But zat is no business of yours, you insolent girl. Now, please go, and be ready when I send for you!" In all her life, Susan had never had to speak to a fellow creature in such a fashion, but she found, in Peg's case, that rudeness was the most effective manner. Grumbling, but obeying nonetheless, Peg bobbed a slight curtsey (which she managed to turn into a sort of insult) and swaggered out of the room.

And Susan, after taking several deep breaths to regain her composure, had set off to look for the cheapest gold band in Calais.

Realizing now that Tom was staring at her in an effort to make out her expression behind her black veils, Susan attempted to shrug off her worries and spoke in a whisper. "It will be all right. It is just that, for all her ignorance, Peg does notice things." She pointed to the ring on her finger. "I had to buy that to convince her I was truly a widow, and yet she will persist in calling me 'miss.' I have to keep reminding her I am *madame*."

Tom's features relaxed in a smile. "If that is all, I shouldn't worry. Rings, to a girl like Peg, are much more significant than major intrigue."

Susan laughed quietly. "She certainly has not noticed anything peculiar about my accent. I've done my best to keep it up, but I sincerely believe she would not know the difference if I left it off entirely."

"Probably not," agreed Tom. "I suppose a person from Yorkshire is as much a foreigner to Peg as a Frenchwoman. Both are to be regarded with the same degree of dislike and suspicion."

Susan did not answer beyond giving a great sigh. Tom's lips twitched in response. "I had better see about the boarding now. Peg is returning with your boxes. It looks a fine day for a sail," he finished cheerfully before leaving her.

It was an extraordinarily fine day. Once aboard, Susan made her way to the starboard deck to look

down at the calm, pale waters as they parted beneath
the ship's bow. Peg had been sent below to watch the
baggage when it became apparent that she meant to
spend the journey at Tom's elbow.

It was a cool winter day and slightly overcast, but
fortunately the wind was steady. Susan thought back
to the only other voyage she had made across the
channel, the time she had brought her father to France
aboard the smuggler's vessel. The wind had been high
that day and the waves fearsome, and she had been
fully occupied in keeping her father cushioned in some
degree of comfort below deck. She had had no chance
to see what a pleasure a channel crossing could be.

In spite of the coolness of the air, she suddenly had
a strong desire to feel the wind upon her cheeks, and
knowing the likelihood of its being her last sea voyage, she raised her veil and faced into the breeze. Tom,
who had been keeping a cautious eye upon her, came
nearer with the intention of watching for anyone who
might try to approach her, but his gaze soon became
fixed upon the image before him. Her lovely features
glowed with warmth in the cool air. And as she lowered her lids to shelter her eyes against the wind, her
silken lashes seemed to ripple softly against the pale-
ness of her skin.

But Tom was interrupted from this pleasant pas-
time when another gentleman, who had been similarly employed, approached Susan from somewhere
beyond his vision. He appeared, from the cut of his
coat, to be an Englishman, and a quick glance reas-

sured Tom that he was not known to him. But before he could intervene to save Susan the inconvenience of speaking to the gentleman, the fellow had reached her side and doffed his hat. Susan noticed him with a start and threw Tom a glance of dismay before lowering her veil again.

"Pardon me, madam, for disturbing you," said the gentleman with just the right degree of diffidence. "I could not help but notice how much you were enjoying the view over the side, and though I sympathize with your pleasure, I felt I ought to caution you against positioning yourself so nearly to the edge. The winds may change suddenly and you might find yourself at a disadvantage." There was nothing improper in his advance, but Tom, whose hair rose inexplicably on the back of his neck, knew with a certainty that the man was only using it as a gambit to make Susan's acquaintance.

She replied with a gracious inclination of the head and moved slightly farther from the side. *"Merci, monsieur,"* she said.

Tom waited anxiously to see if the gentleman, perceiving she was a foreigner, would now have the grace to move off. But the man was in no way discouraged. In fact, his eyes seemed to light up in response.

"Ah, I see that you are French, madam. I have just been enjoying the sights of your lovely capital, which have been so long denied us. I hope our English presence has not been an unwelcome one to you," he added playfully. "But if you are now travelling to my country, perhaps there will be an opportunity for us to repay you for the charming hospitality we've enjoyed among your countrymen." Susan inclined her head again, but did not speak. And immediately the gentleman launched into a speech in fluent French which sent Tom into action.

He approached the gentleman and touched his sleeve. "If I might have a word with you, sir..." he began humbly. The Englishman turned with a frown and then, seeing no one but a servant, turned back to Susan to pursue the conversation.

"Beggin' your pardon for me takin' the liberty to address you, sir," said Tom more insistently this time.

"What is it, fellow?" the gentleman said irritably over his shoulder.

"If I might have a word with you, sir," said Tom again, drawing him back away from Susan, who took the chance to move in the opposite direction. "You see," he explained. "That's my mistress there you were speakin' to, and I sort of have the duty of lookin' after her."

The gentleman's expression changed to amusement, but he was also surprised. "I intend no harm by your mistress, man," he said in a tolerant tone. "Now be a good fellow and run off. I shall do her no harm." He started to turn back, but Tom, thinking quickly, put out an arm to detain him.

The Englishman whipped round angrily as Tom said, "I wouldn't do that if I was you, sir." And before the gentleman could retort he added, "The master wouldn't like it a bit, sir."

"The master?" asked the other, coming up short.

"Yessir."

"But isn't she a widow? I thought I heard someone say she was a widow."

"Oh, no, sir," said Tom now, quite enjoying the other's discomfort. "It's her mother what's just died. That's why she's in mourning. And now she's buried, Mrs. Faringdon's goin' back home to the master."

"I see," said the gentleman, recovering slightly. "Well, as I said, I intend no harm by your mistress, and surely your master cannot object to a little conversation."

"Oh, but that's just it, sir. That's why I felt I ought to speak to you, sir," said Tom in a confidential whisper. "You see, the master's very jealous. He don't like it if anyone speaks to the missus—'cause she's so pretty, sir, as any man can see." He jerked his head back toward Susan with lifted eyebrows. The Englishman followed the direction of his glance and then returned his attention to Tom. His expression was not so confident as before.

"But surely she speaks to casual acquaintances from time to time," he protested.

Tom shook his head vehemently. "Not if she's careful, she don't. If the master gets word of it.... Well, I'd hate to think of it happenin' again."

"Again?"

Tom shuddered violently. The Englishman looked alarmed. "Runs 'em through, sir, he does," said Tom in a terrible whisper. "Time and again. And no matter what the missus says, she can't convince him there was nothin' in it. Just a word or a glance the wrong way sets him off. It's turrible."

The Englishman was staring in horror by now. "But that's insane! The fellow must be mad!"

Tom merely shrugged his shoulders philosophically. "They say he was too long in the colonies. America," he added as if that explained everything. "But anyway, now you see, sir, why I had to speak to you. If the missus has to travel without the master he always sends me along to keep an eye on her, and I have to report back to him about everyone she speaks to—or it's my hide."

The gentleman started. "But in this case, surely..." Then, seemingly mindful of his complete loss of dignity, he drew himself up and regarded Tom haughtily. "This is absurd," he said. "I have not done anything to disturb your mistress and my speaking to her was purely with the intention of preventing her from falling overboard. If there is any need to mention it to your master—and I fail to see any need at all—you must simply tell him that I spoke a word of caution to her, as any gentleman in all charity would have, and passed on." He concluded this speech with an air of having given a command. Then after throwing Susan one more furtive glance, he inclined his head stiffly to her groom and moved away. And to Tom's great enjoyment, the poor man strode rapidly to the far side of the ship and kept his eyes carefully averted for the remainder of the voyage.

Turning his face to hide a gleeful chuckle, Tom suddenly sensed Susan's presence and looked round to find her at his side. "Lord Harleston," she whispered. "What have you done to that poor gentleman? He turned quite pale when he was speaking to you."

"Tom," he reminded her with a respectful bow. "I simply told him that you had a jealous husband who would run him through if he so much as glanced at you."

"You didn't! You're joking, surely! Why, I thought I was supposed to be a widow?"

Tom shrugged cheerfully. "It was the best thing I could think of on such short notice. And it worked. I don't think he'll speak to you again."

"Wretch!" said Susan with a reluctant smile. He was looking decidedly smug, as though he had physically vanquished a rival. It crossed her mind to wonder whether there was not a bit of male possessiveness in that smirk of his and the thought was gratifying. "So now I have to balance two falsehoods among one group of people! Don't forget that Peg thinks I'm a widow. And what if this gentleman should happen to mention my married state to someone else on the journey? It could happen."

"I don't think so," said Tom. "I don't suppose he'll want to say a word about you. But," he added, and his eyes held a certain gleam, "I'm afraid I must ask you not to lift your veil aboard the vessel or I might have to invent countless bouncers to scare away your admirers." He could almost sense the blush which spread quickly over her face.

"Nonsense," she said, but in a trembling voice. His words had implied more of a compliment than a caution. From underneath her veil, Susan could see the amused twinkle in his eyes. "You had better move along now," she reminded him. "It would not do for me to appear to be speaking to my groom too long." Tom answered with an impudent bow and another pull on his forelock.

"No, mum. Your servant, mum," he said. "But I shall be nearby if needed again, mum," he added in an undertone, and Susan could hardly keep from laughing as he backed away from her with servile courtesy.

There were no more incidents aboard the ship to threaten her serenity and within record time, the ship had pulled into harbour at Dover. Here, indeed, she reflected, would come the true test of Lord Harleston's plan as she was obliged to undergo the scrutiny of His Majesty's customs officials.

With Tom behind her carrying her bags and boxes, and Peg swaying close by his side, they made their way slowly through the line as, one by one, the foreign passengers were questioned and harassed and their baggage examined. Earlier, Tom had expressed the wish that her widowed status would awaken the officers' pity and afford her some protection from their well-known tyranny, but as soon as they reached the gates, they could tell this would not be the case.

Whether the official they faced had some personal grievance against Napoleon, or whether he merely felt he had not done his part to defend the Crown in the recent hostilities, they never knew, but he assumed upon reading Susan's passport an immediate gleam of vengeance.

"Mrs. Faringdon, now, is it?" he asked as though her very name were suspicious.

"Yes, *monsieur*," said Susan meekly.

"And a widow, are you?" he asked quickly, trying to catch her off guard.

His apparent suspicion about even the slightest matter did disconcert her and Susan hesitated as she looked quickly about her to make certain that her English admirer was nowhere near to cast doubt on her present story.

"That's right, sir," spoke up Tom to hide her hesitation.

The customs official bristled immediately. He drew himself up to his full height and thrust out his chest, saying, "Nobody's asking *you*, my lad, so just you keep your nose to your business."

Tom answered humbly, "Beggin' your pardon, sir, for the impertinence, but it's just that her English is that bad, sir, that sometimes I has to speak for her." He bowed as he made his apology.

"Humph!" put in Peg saucily. "Not much need she has for you to help *her*." But at the same time, she put her hand to her hip and gave Tom a coy look that said just who *would* be the better for a bit of his help.

"Here, here, now," said the official. "You stop your flirtin', my girl. This is no place for your impudence. Now let me see those bags."

Susan grew suddenly more nervous. Although some of the captain's last belongings were in her boxes, there was nothing that would identify her precisely as Captain Johnstone's daughter. But neither were her possessions such as to convince the official that she was who she pretended to be.

She threw a hasty look at Tom, which he could not see because of her veil, and began to unfasten her first bag with trembling fingers. But his keen eyes perceived the distress in her movements and he whispered a warning as he quickly bent to pick up another bag.

"Remember your cue!"

Susan had no time to wonder what he could mean before he had reached for the other bag and unceremoniously dumped its contents on the ground. She looked up, completely stunned, to find him gazing back at her with his eyes widened in fear.

Suddenly aware of his intentions, she rose ably to the occasion, spurred by her own urgent sense of the need for action.

"*Imbécile!*" she cried, startling them all with the vehemence of her shriek. "*Non, non, non!*" As Tom stepped back and raised his hands defensively to the top of his head, she shrieked even louder and began to flail him with her floppy reticule. *"Idiot!"* she screamed in her best French accent.

"Here, here now, madam!" cried the customs official, seriously alarmed. "Get a hold of yourself! There's no need to carry on like that. The lad couldn't help it!"

But Susan refused to be calmed. She carried on with a series of oaths and insults, which, if they tended to be rather repetitious due to her lack of a suitable vocabulary, were nonetheless convincing. Even Peg, her eyes huge orbs, had the good sense to keep out of her way.

Finally, Tom, occasionally keeping a hand aloft to avoid the random blows of the reticule, managed to stuff the dumped belongings back into the bag and stagger to his feet. With no interference now from the customs official, he gathered up the rest of Susan's bags and was waved onward by the sympathetic officers of the Crown.

Susan followed, muttering an occasional *"idiot"* or *"imbécile"* for the benefit of the officers, who were mopping their brows and exchanging comments about "murderous foreigners" and "Latin temperaments," until they reached the carriage and safety. Then, avoiding as best she could the sight of Tom's woeful countenance as he held the door for her, she climbed into the carriage. Once inside, however, she heaved an enormous sigh of relief before covering her face, veil and all, with both hands to smother the sound of her laughter.

She remained in this position until a sudden lurch called her to the present and she realized that they were on the move. And only then did she remember Peg. The hussy had taken advantage of her mistress's anger to hop aboard the box alongside Tom and even now, if Susan could only have seen, was sitting shockingly close beside him.

But Susan was still elated with her triumph over the customs agents, so without a moment's hesitation, she pulled down the window to the carriage and cried, "Halt!" Tom pulled up the horses with a suddenness which nearly dislodged her from her seat, but she did not let it disturb her. "Peg!" Susan called in a tone which, considering the scene she had just witnessed, the wayward maid did not dare disobey. Within minutes, the carriage had started up again and Peg was inside, riding with her back to the box and a scowl upon her face.

CHAPTER FOUR

THE CARRIAGE BOWLED ALONG at a cheery pace, as if the driver were laughing to himself on the box. Inside, Susan was at pains not to let her shoulders shake or a chuckle escape her lips as she regarded sulky Peg from beneath her widow's veil. The whole episode had left her feeling gay and triumphant, and she could only wish she were up on the box sharing a laugh with Tom instead of continuing the pose for Peg's benefit.

Tom! She caught herself up short. *Lord Harleston to you,* she reminded herself, feeling suddenly less cheerful. The next time she saw him would be nearly the last, for they planned to let Peg down in London and travel on until they reached her governess's house next day. Susan had protested the lack of rest for Lord Harleston in such a rigorous schedule, but he had laughed and reminded her of his much more Spartan life in the Peninsula. It would be nothing to him after enduring days in the saddle. They would stop along the road to break their journey and he would enjoy getting a bite with the ostlers and coachmen in the public rooms.

Peg shifted complainingly in the seat, as though she were used to a more luxurious form of travel. Susan frowned at the tiresome girl, her sense of humour momentarily gone. At least she would soon be rid of her! That was one thing she need not regret.

But she had to admit to herself that she would regret losing Lord Harleston's company. She had never experienced anything quite so pleasurable as planning this escapade with him, despite her early reservations. She smiled rather wistfully at the thought of hay in his wind-tossed hair. It seemed so natural, somehow, to think of him up there on the box, taking her to safety—not so much as her groom, but just taking care of her. How easily she had come to think of him as Tom. But of course she mustn't! Lord Harleston had already risked too much by embroiling himself in her troublesome affairs. She must not think of him as her friend. Friendship with a woman who was wanted by the authorities could only harm him. Susan tried to think of the pleasure of seeing her governess again, but in spite of her sincere devotion to that lady, found it hard to imagine her face. A pair of laughing, brown-gold eyes kept swimming in the way.

Up on the box, Tom whistled to himself and cracked his whip to urge on a sluggish wheeler. The leaders' pace suited his humour to a T. In case the authorities had somehow leapt to a suspicion of Susan's identity, he had chosen to detour south and west toward the Folkstone road to London. It would add a bit to their time, but should give a measure of security.

Without Peg's sultry eyes upon him, he was free to indulge an inclination to laugh over the morning's work. Even the memory of the male passenger on board ship brought a smile to his lips. The fellow had really been taken with Susan—*Miss Johnstone, that is,* Tom reminded himself. But who wouldn't be?

He remembered her exquisite profile as she had gazed blissfully out to sea, the wind ruffling the gentle curls at her ears. Something stirred within him and he had to recall himself to the business of guiding the horses before they bolted from the sudden tension in his hands. It was too bad, he reflected, that they could not ride in comfort together rather than separated by the etiquette of the coach. Perhaps when they reached London and got rid of Peg, some other arrangement might be made. He searched his mind for a different solution, but could not think of one which would accomplish their mission and still serve the proprieties. Damn the proprieties!

It might be nice if Peg and she could change places, he thought fancifully. Certainly the servant girl had had no worries about her reputation when she had joined him on the box. He could still feel the warmth on his left side where she had pressed herself against him. Quite a handful, that one, but not for him. He would never consider using his masquerade to deceive the poor wench. Not that he thought a little deceit would trouble Peg overmuch, but if she were with them much longer, her overtures might become a problem. He could not blame her for making the most of her situation, for as long as she was in service she would be closely watched and forbidden to be with a man. She was just taking her chance on finding a husband before it was too late. With her buxom figure she should not have much trouble.

But *his* tastes ran more to dark-haired, willowy ladies, with a gentle manner and a courageous heart. He would be saying goodbye to Susan in a matter of hours, he realized, and yet here he was urging the horses on to the end of their journey. He started to pull them up, but came to the conclusion it would not do him much good. It would only prolong getting rid of Peg. And Susan could not share the box with him, on any account. He must do what he could to protect her name.

Of course, the next task would be to seek a pardon for her defiance of the law. He would work on that as soon as he resumed his own identity. Lord Harleston had little fear he would be unable to clear her somehow, but it might take time. He had already left word with his staff not to expect him back for several weeks. He would stay in London, working toward her pardon, and, of course, travelling back and forth to give Susan reports of his progress.

The first person to approach would be the Prince's equerry. Thank heavens Captain Johnstone had been such a dandy, for the Prince, if he recalled, had admired his style of dress. And the captain had never been so unwise as to criticize his sovereign's less successful attempts. Captain Johnstone's heroism in the Peninsula, too, should go a long way in his favour. Prinny was a sentimentalist. He had been known to break down in tears upon hearing a sad story. Surely he could be made to forgive the rash act of a tender-hearted daughter upon seeing her father, a national hero, near death.

Yes, he must request an audience with the Regent as soon as possible. It would be then just a matter of weeks. Meanwhile, he could be priming the Regent's advisers to smooth his way, and it would not hurt to broach the subject with Lady Hertford, the Prince's current object of affection.

Tom had just reached this point in his thinking when something ahead on the road captured his attention. It appeared to be an overturned carriage, and as he approached he spied two figures seated beside it in the ditch.

He pulled up the chaise and called back to Susan. "There seems to be an accident up ahead, madam. Shall I stop the carriage?"

Susan stuck her head out the window and uttered a little cry at the forlorn sight in front of her. "Oh, yes, Tom. Zat is, *oui, oui, bien sûr!*"

The carriage and its inhabitants, as they saw when they came nearer, made a rather peculiar picture. The coach itself, enormous in size, was covered in black silk and, although it might have been the first style of elegance more than fifty years before, was now something of a relic. It appeared to have lost an axle; the wheel must have collapsed. Indeed, the whole contraption appeared to be crumbling before their very eyes.

Beside it were two elderly people. A lady of unbelievable antiquity (and also in black silk) sat in some disarray with her feet in the ditch. Her companion, a servant of some kind, was, if possible, even older and more fragile. They both were clearly shaken by the disaster.

"Oh, you poor dears!" cried Susan, scarcely waiting for Tom to hand her down. A squeeze from Tom's hand reminded her to play her role, so she hastily added, *"Les pauvres!* What 'as 'appened?" She lifted her veil in order to speak to the aged victims.

The two elderly people struggled to their feet, each endeavouring to help the other, and Tom and Susan hurried to give their assistance.

"How good of you to stop," said the lady in a slightly quavering voice. "Our carriage overturned, as you can see. I cannot think what happened. It is my best travelling coach."

Susan glanced back at the coach with some surprise and avoided Tom's eye. "Of course you cannot. Such a 'andsome carriage as it was—I am certain somes'ing can be done for it. But we must get you to a place of comfort. I am Madame Suzanne Faringdon." She had decided rather abruptly that she could no longer pretend to have a limited vocabulary. The situation demanded complete sentences at the very least. Tom would have to be satisfied with a slight Gallic intonation.

"And I am Lady Mewhinny, my dear," replied the old lady. "That is mew, like a cat, and whinny, like a horse. Mewhinny. Are you from Scotland?"

Susan started and, as Tom turned away to hide a smile, replied in a rather wounded voice, "*Non, non,* my lady. I am French. My 'usband, 'e was an Englishman." She hoped a slight exaggeration would settle the matter.

"And you are widowed," Lady Mewhinny guessed sadly. "And you such a pretty young woman. I am a widow, too, my dear, though Sir William died when I was somewhat older than you are now. Could your man take a look at my carriage to see what needs to be done to right it? Perhaps we can go along in it."

Susan eyed the miserable heap of wood and black silk doubtfully but, trying to make her request sound like an order, asked Tom to do his best. Then she offered Lady Mewhinny her arm to take her back to Lord Harleston's carriage where she might be seated more comfortably.

The frail lady (eighty-five if she was a day, thought Susan) made slow progress back to the chaise. "I cannot think what is the matter," she said finally. "I scarcely seem to know my own limbs."

"You 'ave been dreadfully shaken!" replied Susan, aching with pity for the poor lady. "It is no wonder you are not quite right."

"I suppose so," Lady Mewhinny agreed. "To tell the truth, I do not think Vigor feels quite the thing, either. I hardly like to ask him to help your groom."

"Vigor?" asked Susan blankly.

"Yes, my groom. He is directly descended from the Roman invaders on both sides," she explained proudly. "He is from Sussex, you see. His mother's name was Venus and his father's, Avis. You can see it in his nose, of course."

"'is nose?"

"Of course, my dear. Why surely you must have noticed his Roman nose!"

Susan looked back over her shoulder at the thin, stooped creature hovering over the doomed carriage but managed to keep the smile from her voice. "I am afraid I did not, Lady Mewhinny. But I was so concerned about you, I must 'ave been raz'er unobservant."

Lady Mewhinny laid a wasted hand on Susan's and patted it kindly. "Aren't you a dear," she said. Her voice had lost its quavering quality. "You must not worry about me; I am sure your man will have the carriage righted shortly."

But no sooner had Lady Mewhinny been settled comfortably in Susan's chaise than she was proven wrong. When Tom stepped up to the window to make his report Susan saw that his breeches had taken on a vast quantity of mud.

"I'm afraid it's no use, milady," he said in the humblest of tones. "It's going to take more than one man to set your coach to rights."

"Oh, bother!" exclaimed Lady Mewhinny. "Now we shall be delayed."

Susan looked at Lord Harleston and noticed a streak of mud across his forehead. He was holding up magnificently, but she could see the relief in his expression. He obviously thought they were about to resolve the episode. But they could not leave Lady Mewhinny and Vigor here.

Directing Tom a subtly pleading glance, Susan said, "You must let us convey you somewhere, Lady Mewhinny. Was your destination 'ere in ze vicinity?"

"Oh, no, I could not trouble you to do that!" protested the older woman. "You were on a journey of your own. I would not think of interrupting it more than I already have!"

"But zat is absurd!" cried Susan, more than ever wishing to help. The frail lady's courage touched her deeply. "We were just on our way to London. But zere is no urgency; we 'ave no business zere. A slight delay will not inconvenience us in ze least." She could sense the widening of his lordship's eyes.

Lady Mewhinny offered no further protest. "Then I accept," she said. "It is most kind of you to offer. To tell the truth, I had worried about Vigor." She lowered her voice to a near whisper. "He is not as young as he used to be, though you might not think it. You see, he was already in Sir William's service when I married him in 1749."

Susan's eyes opened with incredulity and Tom put a quick hand to his mouth to stifle a cough. "*Non*, I should never s'ink it," said Susan hastily. "Now where may we set you down?"

Lady Mewhinny sat a bit straighter in her seat and placed her hands on her lap with a curiously authoritative gesture. "That will be quite simple. My estates are in Sussex, near Heathfield. Do not be concerned if your man doesn't know the way," she added at Susan's look of surprise. "Vigor shall ride up on the box beside him and direct him. Then I hope you will be so good as to accept my hospitality while your man comes back for my carriage."

Susan opened her mouth in shock. Had she really heard that correctly? Was Lady Mewhinny proposing such an imposition on a peer of the realm? She started to protest, "But Lord..." and was fortunately cut off by another cough from Tom. "... Tom," she finished lamely, directing a helpless look in his direction.

"Lord Tom?" repeated Lady Mewhinny, turning her head back and forth between them in confusion.

Tom stepped quickly into the breach. "Yes, milady. Lord Tom. That's what the master had a way of calling me. He said I got above my station from time to time."

Lady Mewhinny inclined her head with good humour. "All the better," she said, suddenly cheerful. "You will need a touch of authority to get any assistance from the louts in this part of the Weald. They are not so energetic as we are in Sussex. Now let us be off, shall we? It is over thirty miles."

Susan and Tom looked at each other speechlessly. Thirty miles and the day was almost gone! Then Susan realized that her face must have betrayed her anguish for Tom gave her a smile of reassurance before bowing to both ladies.

"Certainly, milady. Madam," he finished, pulling his forelock for Susan's benefit.

Within a few minutes, he had helped his ancient guide onto the box and they were on their way.

Susan sank back against the cushioned sides of the carriage Lord Harleston had provided. Heedless of Lady Mewhinny's presence, she pulled her veil down over her eyes and closed them tightly. What had she done now? She should never have allowed Lord Harleston to talk her into this mad escapade. Look at the muddle they were in now, and all because she was too impulsive to think before she acted. He would never forgive her after this day's work. Or at least, she thought, remembering his reassuring smile, he certainly ought not to.

The carriage rolled faster and faster over the bumpy roads. There was no direct route to Heathfield, it seemed, for they had to take every market road that twisted between Ashford and Lady Mewhinny's estate. It soon grew dark and Tom had to stop at an inn to obtain extra lanterns to light the route. Susan and Lady Mewhinny used the stop to freshen themselves and have dinner before climbing back into the carriage. Lady Mewhinny insisted upon paying for their fare, but Susan found it hard to eat, wondering if Tom were getting something to sustain him through the night. She gave orders to the effect that the servants should be fed, but had no idea how well they would be carried out. Peg, who had offered no assistance throughout the day, was sent to see to it that the others got to eat. From the gleam in Peg's eye, Susan felt secure that she would at least find Tom. The thought was not particularly comforting.

Once back inside the carriage, Susan vowed to herself that she would not go to sleep while Lord Harleston could not do the same. Lady Mewhinny dozed comfortably in a corner, seemingly indifferent to the bouncing of the chaise. Peg, although still rather sulky about riding backward, seemed less petulant than before. Susan glanced at her from time to time, wondering what attention, if any, the girl had had from Tom. It would not seem natural to Peg for him to ignore her, she well knew, but she wondered to what lengths Lord Harleston would feel obliged to go for verisimilitude.

It had been a long day. Susan had risen at five o'clock to make ready for their voyage, and no amount of resolve could counter that fact. To her later mortification, she dropped off to sleep and made little attempt to keep awake when little jerks of the carriage brought her abruptly to herself.

When she finally awoke, it was near dawn the next day and Tom had slowed the horses' pace to turn into a long alley. Lady Mewhinny was regarding her complacently. She seemed fully restored from her accident, despite a journey which would have caused many women to take to their beds.

"Ah, I see you are awake," she said, smiling. "And just when we're arriving. This is the lane to Kittycall Manor. Your man seems to have found it without one wrong turn."

"Kittycall?" asked Susan dazedly, forgetting her accent.

"Yes," said Lady Mewhinny with a chuckle. "Sir William's people had quite a sense of humour. It is on account of the name, of course. Mew, you know."

"Oh, quite," said Susan. She fumbled in her reticule for a comb and straightened her hair as well as she could without a mirror. She was dreading the sight of Tom and wanted to look her best when she faced him. It was certain to be the last time.

Peg was still snoring as they drew up before the manor and Susan had to rouse her before they could assist Lady Mewhinny to her feet. The house was an impressive Palladian structure with three great sections joined in the shape of a U, but Susan paid it scant attention. Her eyes sought Tom in the crowd of aged servants who seemed suddenly to envelop them.

Tom had descended from the carriage and was leaning tiredly against one of the wheels, but he straightened as she alighted. Their eyes met above the heads of the servants and Susan winced at the redness in his. He stepped forward to meet her just as Lady Mewhinny took her arm.

"Might I have a word with you, Mrs. Faringdon?" he said hurriedly.

"Of course, T-Tom," said Susan, glancing at Lady Mewhinny helplessly. "What is it?"

Lord Harleston looked at the elderly lady and back to Susan, giving an almost imperceptible shrug of his shoulders. It couldn't be helped.

"I just wanted to reassure you, madam, that I'll be back with the carriage as soon as possible. You needn't worry." The look in his eyes spoke volumes.

Lord Harleston's concern for her nearly wrung Susan's heart. "Oh, you must not be worried about me, Tom," she said earnestly. "I am certain I shall be fine. But you must get some rest," she added, "and somes'ing to eat before setting out. Must 'e not, Lady Mewhinny?" she pleaded as she saw the slight shake to his head.

"Yes, Tom. There's a good fellow," said Lady Mewhinny. "Be off with you now and Vigor will tell you how to go on. Bates," she said, calling to her elderly butler who seemed nevertheless a child in comparison to his mistress, "see to it that Mrs. Faringdon's groom is given something to eat before he sets out."

"Yes, milady," said Bates with wounded dignity. He clearly did not stand in need of instruction.

"And now let us go in, my dear," said Lady Mewhinny, sweeping Susan forward briskly. "You will need some refreshment after your journey."

Susan managed a wistful look back over her shoulder at Tom before she was handed to the housekeeper and guided to her room.

CHAPTER FIVE

THE WALK DOWN the bedroom corridor took longer than it ought to have because Lady Mewhinny's housekeeper suffered from rheumatism and could only walk at a snail's pace. It hurt Susan to watch her and she vowed not to require the poor woman to make the journey again on her account. It seemed to her there was not a person under sixty-five on the staff, although apparently Lady Mewhinny and Vigor had already outlived one generation of servants.

Her room, however, came as something of a shock. It was furnished in the height of the rococo style, with the sumptuous curves of that particular style evident in all the furniture. The ceilings were painted in soft pastels edged in gilt. Elaborately framed paintings of pastoral seductions and pink-breasted nudes covered the walls, and as Susan approached them rather fearfully, she detected the signatures of both Watteau and Fragonard. Clearly, despite the outdated fashion of the chamber, Sir William had possessed a considerable fortune.

"Cooo!" came a voice from behind her. Peg had been sent to find her mistress. "Now this is something like." The miserable girl walked slowly into the room, staring openmouthed at each of the voluptuous canvases. She tittered at the figure of a reclining gentleman who seemed to be reaching out to touch his lady's breast.

Susan coloured in embarrassment. "Zat will do, Peg!" she said sharply, "You may help me unpack later. For ze moment, I wish to retire. I will ring for you when I need you."

"Oll right, miss," said Peg, not unwilling to depart. "But 'oo I'm a goin' to talk to, I don't know. Them's all older 'an me grandfer downstairs."

"You may go, Peg," said Susan wearily.

The girl went at that, but not before she had stopped in front of another of the canvases and giggled again. Her hips seemed to sway more pronouncedly as she left the room, as though something in the paintings had acted as an inspiration to them.

Susan lay down gratefully upon the fattened comforters. The bed was so luxurious, despite the age of its coverings, that she had little fear of not being able to rest. The previous day had been exhausting in more than one way. But as she lay there, trying not to think of Peg, or worry about Tom, she could not manage to sleep. Finally, she realized that a strange noise, coming from so far away she had not been fully aware of it, was disturbing her tranquility.

She rose in her bed and listened carefully. Briefly it was gone, but soon again she heard a faint shrieking sound. It was rather eerie. She thought for a moment it might be the wind, but there was no wind to speak of that day. She lay down again and she was trying to dismiss it from her mind, when there came a tap upon her door.

Susan jumped and then rose quickly from the bed to answer it. Peg, she knew, would not have the decency to knock. To her surprise, it proved to be Lady Mewhinny, whom she had supposed to be laid out on her bed for the rest of the day.

But her ladyship, at Susan's invitation, stepped into the room with a liveliness Susan could only envy.

"I've just come to see how you were getting on, my dear. I hope you are comfortably settled."

Susan thanked her, assuring her of her perfect delight, but protesting the effort it must have caused her hostess to look in on her.

"Nonsense, my dear" was her ladyship's answer. "I am happy to see you installed. This was my room, you see. Sir William had it fitted out for me when we were newly married. I've always loved it, but I chose another room shortly after he died. Somehow it seemed the right thing to do," she added vaguely.

She turned to the dressing table and said, "Did you see the shell mirror and brush he gave me? You must use them if you like. And anything else you have need of while you are here. Bates said you did not have much baggage with you."

Susan flushed and tried to hide her confusion. "*Non* . . . you see, we were not planning a protracted journey."

"Yes, I see. Well, please use anything you like. There are some clothes in the chest which ought to fit you reasonably well if you run short. They have been kept in good repair, so you need not fear you would look shabby."

"S'ank you, my lady," said Susan hastily. "I shall manage quite all right." She had visions of herself dressed as Madame Pompadour with a wig, pannier and patches. "Zere is one s'ing I did wish to ask you, zough. Do you 'ear a strange noise?"

Lady Mewhinny opened her eyes widely and cocked her head to one side like a little bird. "No. I cannot say that I do. And my hearing is quite acute." She looked at Susan expectantly.

"Zen it must be my imagination." Susan frowned, shaking her head to dismiss it. "Please do not give it anoz'er s'ought, Lady Mewhinny."

The elderly lady took her hand and patted it kindly. "You must call me Kitty, dear. My name is Catherine, you know. And I shall call you Susan. We are both widows and, I think, are very like in some ways.

"I remember my own grief after Sir William died," she continued. "But I did not give into it and I fancy Sir William would have wanted it that way. You must not bury yourself, you know. Life goes on."

Tears of gratitude and mortification came to Susan's eyes. "Oh, Lady Mewhinny—Kitty. You're so very kind."

"Nonsense, my dear. It is such a pleasure for me to have a new friend—and of the human variety, too. I had best let you have your rest,'' she finished cheerily. And with another pat of the hand, she was gone.

Susan was so touched by Kitty's kindness and at the same time guilt-ridden to be deceiving her that the strangeness of her ladyship's last remarks did not strike her immediately. When it did, she merely thought that Lady Mewhinny had a rather sharp sense of humour to be referring to her collection of aged servants as if they were a menagerie. What other explanation could there be?

She lay down again upon the bed and managed finally, despite the faint shrieking in her ears, to sleep. Unfortunately, her concerns about Lord Harleston were so much in her mind that her dreams were fitful. She dreamed that she waited and waited anxiously for Tom to return, but when she finally searched for him and found him, he was buried to his waist in mud. She wanted desperately to grasp him and pull him out, but could not bring herself to put her arms around him for fear he might think her forward. It was a most disquieting dream.

When Susan awoke, she found it was near noon. Lady Mewhinny must have left word she was not to be disturbed, for no one had come to bring her breakfast. She leapt from the bed and ran to the window to look for Tom. Her dreams of him were still vivid, and she had some notion of checking to see whether he were stuck in the garden, but all that greeted her eyes were the neat rows of Lady Mewhinny's vegetables and roses.

Having still some hope of speaking to Lord Harleston before he could leave, she dressed quickly and went in search of the public rooms. The house was straightforward in design and had no twisting corridors to confuse her, so she came rapidly to the central section. Bates, Lady Mewhinny's butler, was just coming out of one of the rooms with a tray when she rounded the corner.

Stepping quickly to catch up with him, Susan called out, "Bates! Oh, Bates!"

He must not have heard, for he turned away and walked with stately dignity in the opposite direction. Supposing that he might be slightly deaf, Susan gathered her skirt in one hand and ran lightly after him, still calling.

As she closed with him, however, Susan suddenly came within his hearing, and he turned quickly in time to see her running. She halted breathlessly before him, not a little embarrassed to be caught in such a manner.

"Yes, madam," he said, showing no sign of surprise at being thus accosted.

"Oh, Bates!" Susan breathed anxiously. "I was wondering whez'er someone might be sent to ze stables wiz an instruction for my groom. I would like to speak to 'im before 'e sets out again."

Bates bowed stiffly, as if with disdain for her inferior awareness. "To the best of my knowledge, madam, the said person left several hours ago," he said. "Right after breaking his fast, if I am not mistaken. But I will enquire if you wish." His tone suggested she would be greatly in error to doubt any information she received from *him*.

Susan shrank, but did not give in. "Yes, please do, Bates. S'ank you."

Bates bowed again. This time not so terribly. He seemed to gain respect for someone he could not crush. "I shall see to it immediately, madam. Lady Mewhinny is in the breakfast parlour. If you like, I shall conduct you to her and have something brought up for you shortly."

Susan released a breath gratefully and smiled. "S'ank you, Bates. Zat would be delightful."

She was shown into a room which bore the same style as the room in which she slept, although the paintings were, in general, more modest than those in her boudoir. Lady Mewhinny was seated at the table sipping tea and reading a stack of papers at her side. From the remnants on her plate, Susan could see she had a remarkably hearty appetite for one her age.

"Good afternoon, my dear. I see you've had your rest."

Susan greeted her and affirmed it, mentioning that Bates was already seeing to her breakfast.

"I was just finishing a small luncheon," said Kitty. "I breakfasted earlier and got on with my work. So much to catch up on after a journey from home, you know," she added at Susan's look of surprise.

Her ladyship appeared to be completely recovered from her accident of the day before. Indeed, she showed no sign of having had one. It was amazing, nonetheless, thought Susan, that a woman of Lady Mewhinny's age and fortune should not have a steward to take care of her business. Surely she did, yet the stack of papers before her suggested Lady Mewhinny was quite closely involved with her business affairs.

Susan's breakfast was brought in on a tray with a number of journals, so she was able to eat in quiet while her ladyship continued her work. But the shrieking in Susan's ears had not abated; in fact, it seemed rather louder. She was just beginning to wonder whether she had not developed a case of nerves, when the screams increased so sharply as to make her drop her cup and jump to her feet.

Lady Mewhinny looked up curiously. "Something wrong, my dear?"

Susan gazed at her in disbelief. "Surely you heard that, my lady! It was the peculiar sound I was asking about."

Lady Mewhinny shook her head in perplexity. "I didn't hear anything peculiar, my dear."

Susan struggled to maintain her calm as the shrieks grew louder again. "I do not like to suggest it, my lady—Kitty," she amended, "But per'aps your 'earing is not quite what it was, for ze most dreadful shrieking is coming from zat direction." She pointed toward the farthest wing of the house where she had not yet been.

To her great relief, Lady Mewhinny chuckled. "Oh, I am so sorry, Susan, my love. You are talking about the west wing! Of course I hear it. But I am so used to it, you see, that I do not consider it strange at all. And you did ask if I heard anything peculiar.''

Susan waited expectantly, happy, at least, to know she was not imagining things.

''Those are my pensioners,'' said Lady Mewhinny placidly.

Susan's eyes widened in alarm. ''Your pensioners?''

''Yes, my dear. It is so silly of me. I forgot to tell you about my charity. I care for some one hundred or more unfortunates who have been cruelly abandoned. It is their behaviour, you know. People tire of them when they begin to shriek and bite and tear the curtains and so on. But here they are well cared for.''

Susan swallowed and said weakly, ''Zat's quite admirable,'' before looking toward the door in the impossible hope that Tom had already returned.

Lady Mewhinny glanced at Susan's plate and saw she had finished. ''Would you like to see them?'' she asked brightly.

Susan choked on her last bite of food. ''Certainly,'' she said when she could. ''*Sometime*. Zat would be lovely. But I must not take you from your work.''

''There is no time like the present,'' said Lady Mewhinny, rising. Susan thought she spoke in a remarkably cheery tone. She rose to her feet, wondering how she would react to seeing rooms full of lunatics. She knew that others derived considerable amusement from seeing them; Bedlam was quite the tourist attraction. But Susan had never been tempted. The thought of such miserable humanity was always too much for her tender heart and she doubted she could face them without enduring tortured dreams for the rest of her life.

Lady Mewhinny led her briskly down the hall which opened into the west wing. The screams and shrieks grew steadily louder as though the inmates were enjoying a competition of sorts. Susan wondered if any of them were, by contrast, moribund, and if they were, how they managed to survive the noise.

Lady Mewhinny stopped before a room with large double doors. Then, as she directed the footman to open them, Susan said a brief, silent prayer. She pleaded not to be so overcome with pity for the miserable inmates that she would there and then pledge her life to their service.

The doors opened and her nostrils were assailed by an overpoweringly foul odour, which would have added to her horror if she had not immediately caught sight of the inhabitants within.

"Monkeys!" she cried in relief. They were monkeys. At first, as their shrieks rose as if to greet them, Susan thought there must be hundreds of them. They were enclosed in enormous cages so big that they hardly seemed to be cages at all, and the creatures were bounding about and hurling themselves against the sides as if they were crazed with joy.

Lady Mewhinny moved about and among them uttering soothing sounds. She had picked up a basket as she entered the room, and at the moment was dipping into it for small pieces of fruit which she fed to her "pensioners" through the bars. Susan could now see that it was their delight in her visit which had caused such an uproar, for they eventually calmed as those who received their bit of fruit ran off to enjoy it in relative peace.

"Would you like to feed one of them?" asked Lady Mewhinny, offering Susan a rather mushy tidbit.

Devoutly hoping her hostess had not heard her first outburst, Susan hastened to take it from her and pushed it through the bars. A little brown creature with an elfin face, black hands and feet came shyly toward her along his perch. She was surprised at how gently he took the present from her, but even more so by his subsequent gestures, for he bowed repeatedly and touched his head as if he were removing his hat.

"Oh, look!" she cried. "'E's s'anking me! 'Ow darling! Did you teach 'im zat, Kitty?"

"Oh, no, my dear," said Lady Mewhinny, shaking her head sadly. "I would not have time with so many creatures to care for, though I do try to give them each some special attention. They need it, you know. They must have affection or they die. No, this one belonged to a hurdy-gurdy man evidently, for he has been trained to do tricks for his supper. I don't demand it of him, naturally, but he does not understand that."

"'Ow did you come by zem all?" asked Susan in a wondering tone. She had completely recovered from her earlier misconception and was now full of curiosity.

Lady Mewhinny explained. "Well, as I told you, these are my pensioners. I am the founder of the Society for Abandoned Simians. I thought I mentioned that to you, my dear."

"Not precisely," said Susan, hiding a smile at her own foolishness. "But now I understand. Only why are zere so many abandoned simians? One would s'ink zere 'ad never been so many in all of England."

"Oh, but there were, dear," said Lady Mewhinny. "You have no idea how popular it was when I was younger to have a monkey of your own. All the most fashionable ladies wanted one. And, of course, it was the merchants who brought them so their daughters had to have them, too. Why, if you didn't have a monkey from East India, a lapdog from Vigo or a page from Genoa, you were not quite the thing! But then they tired of them, you see, just as if they were a type of fan or periwig to be disposed of. Besides, they are quite demanding little creatures and they bite if they have a tantrum, which did not suit my lady long. Scores of them were handed about from one owner to another, until eventually no one wanted them. And the poor little monkeys grow morose when they are not wanted. They are quite intelligent; they know, you see."

"But . . ." Susan tried to phrase her question tactfully, "do zey live so very long? I should s'ink you must 'ave 'ad most of zese for quite some time, zen."

Lady Mewhinny laughed lightly. "Oh, these are not all orphans from my girlhood. Oh, my no. Though they do live longer than most animals their size. Oh, no. Most of these are children, and grandchildren, of my first pensioners, as I like to call them. They are unhappy if they aren't with other monkeys, you see, so they do tend to multiply. And I still get the occasional pet who is no longer wanted. I put advertisements in the journals."

"Ah, I see," said Susan, though she did not really. To think of this multitude being left free to multiply! How many might there become! And who was to carry on after Lady Mewhinny left this earth? Would they all be allowed to starve?

"Zis society, Lady Mewhinny . . . Kitty," she asked, "are zere many members?"

Her ladyship nodded smilingly. "Why, yes. I fancy there must be quite a number of us now. Perhaps you would like to join us, dear?"

Susan started and flushed ashamedly. Then she asserted warmly, "I would love to, Kitty, and I shall—as soon as I can. But my funds are not mine to manage, you see."

"How irksome for you!" said Kitty sympathetically. "I should never have forgiven Sir William if he had left me so uncomfortably, but he put everything in my hands. He trusted me to care for myself completely."

"Zat was fortunate," said Susan, putting an end to the subject. She did not want to get into a comparative discussion with Lady Mewhinny over the merits and defects of their deceased husbands. Invention was not one of her strongest points, nor a pleasure. Instead, they walked on awhile with Lady Mewhinny stroking this monkey or that. After a time, Susan learned that the odour became more tolerable, and she noticed the cages were remarkably clean. A sizable staff was needed to feed the animals and tidy the cages apparently, but Lady Mewhinny did not seem to feel the burden.

After they had visited the inhabitants of another room down the hall, Lady Mewhinny turned to Susan and said, "I must leave you now, my love. I have a meeting with the local grain merchant. I fear he has been passing off some inferior grain on my monkeys and I must take him to task for it. Feel free to wander about if you wish—any attention you give them can only do them good—and I shall see you at dinner. We dine at six."

Susan released her immediately to her business and tarried awhile longer amongst the chattering inmates. Their tiny hands reached out of the cages to touch her and she gave them her fingers to hold, much as she would have to a baby. It was easy to see how someone as loving as Lady Mewhinny could become devoted to these endearing creatures. But it was a little mad, surely?

Susan had asked tactfully and learned that her ladyship had no children. Perhaps if she had, she would not have developed her odd passion for monkeys. Susan tried not to think about their eventual end when Lady Mewhinny would not be around to support them. There was some heir, she supposed, who would do away with them all, or sell them to a commercial menagerie. They would be found places in the circus or zoological gardens, but of course they would not be so well treated there... Susan stopped herself with a shake. *I must not let myself be caught up with the welfare of these animals!* she told herself sternly. *I must concentrate on maintaining this ridiculous pose until Tom can come to fetch me.*

She sighed, wondering how Lord Harleston was doing and how long it would take him to see to the carriage and return. At least he would not have to keep up the pretense of being a groom while he was not with her, so he might, at this very moment, be resting while lackeys from the smithy's shop righted the ancient vehicle.

Susan comforted herself with this thought the rest of the day. At dinner she learned more about Lady Mewhinny's charitable institution and found herself growing more and more fond of her ladyship. Kitty, in spite of a long day of attending to matters, was no less concerned with Susan's comfort than she had been at the start of the day. It was a strange feeling, and a wonderful one, thought Susan, to be the object of so much loving concern. No one save Miss Irons had ever shown her such affection, and nothing could exceed Lady Mewhinny's eagerness to see her happy. What a wonderful mother she would have made, Susan could not help thinking. Even her eccentricity could not diminish the effect of her kindness.

In the course of that day and the one which followed, Susan forgot, at times, to sound French, but Lady Mewhinny did not seem to notice. The one flaw in her intelligence seemed to be that she did not have an ear for languages, as she confided to Susan the next evening at the dinner table.

"I am so glad you speak English as well as you do, Susan," she said, "for I was never much good at French. My French master despaired of ever teaching me a single word, and as for Italian..." She left off with a laugh.

"Zat is too bad, Kitty," answered Susan, scarcely hiding her relief. "I would 'ave loved to converse wiz you in my own tongue. But you must not let it concern you. I am quite used to speaking English. My 'usband, you remember..."

"Of course, my dear. And isn't it fortunate for us both he was an Englishman. Otherwise we might never have met. Now where was it you said his estates are situated?"

Susan froze for an instant, trying to remember the story she and Lord Harleston had agreed upon. In his absence, she had strived to keep his image at a distance, but she had not intended to forget all his instructions. In truth, as the time passed, she had begun to worry about him, wondering when he would return. Her mind was distracted, and she could not think clearly. She was about to issue a vaguely worded answer to Lady Mewhinny's question, when a footman approached the table.

"Excuse me, milady," he said, directing his comments to Lady Mewhinny, "but madam's servant has just returned with the carriage and said she requested to be told as soon as he arrived."

Susan sprang to her feet eagerly. "Lord...! Tom!" she corrected herself. "I must have a word with him."

Lady Mewhinny regarded her, her eyes mildly curious. "Surely you could send a message, dear."

"Oh, no!" Susan protested vehemently. "Zat is, you see...zat's not ze way we do it. We French, I mean. We always speak to our servants directly. It is a vestige from ze revolution, you see. We dare not trust anyone to carry out our wishes unless we 'ave seen zem for ourselves."

Lady Mewhinny looked puzzled, but did not ask for further explanations. "It shall certainly be as you wish then, dear. Far be it from me to suggest otherwise, having not lived through such a horror. But could it not wait until you have finished your meal?"

Susan blushed with embarrassment and sank back into her chair. She knew she had seemed more eager than the situation warranted, but she could hardly wait to see Lord Harleston again.

"Of course, my lady. 'Ow silly of me. It was my earnest desire not to impose upon you any longer zat made me jump in 'aste. I shall 'ave to instruct Tom to ready our carriage for tomorrow."

"Oh, must you leave?" asked Lady Mewhinny sadly. "I have so enjoyed your company."

Susan felt ready tears spring to her eyes. "And so 'ave I, Kitty. I 'ave never felt so at 'ome. But we, zat is, *I* 'ave a commitment, and I 'ave already stayed too long."

"I understand, dear," said Lady Mewhinny kindly. "But I hope you will come to visit me again soon."

"You are very kind," Susan answered noncommittally. She wished it were in her power to do otherwise.

She sat uncomfortably throughout the rest of dinner, trying not to appear too anxious, yet yearning to go and find Tom. Fortunately, Lady Mewhinny was not a finicky eater. She seemed to require loads of nourishment to feed her energy, but disposed of it very rapidly. Soon she got up from the table and Susan was free to leave it. So, bidding her hostess good-night, she went in search of Tom.

CHAPTER SIX

SUSAN FOUND THE STABLES with the assistance of a footman and, dismissing him, entered the vast, dark building. Lanterns were burning, hung up along the walls a safe distance from the stacks of straw, but no one seemed to be inside minding the horses. What horses there were, she had to admit, required little care, for the huge room was almost empty of animal life. Lady Mewhinny had little reason for keeping a large stable.

Susan began to tiptoe about, looking over and around the empty stalls for signs of Tom.

"Lord Harleston," she whispered loudly into the silence, her footsteps muted by the layers of straw. "Lord Harleston, where are you?"

From behind a nearby wall, a deep chuckle greeted her, followed by Lord Harleston's voice saying, "That is a very strange way to address your groom, madam."

Susan peeped over the wall and was shocked to find Tom lying in a bed of hay, looking for all the world as if he had been in a cockfight. His clothes were soiled and torn, and she spied several scratches on his face and hands.

"Lord Harleston! What happened?" she cried, coming around the wall to sink beside him in the straw. She had to restrain herself from putting out a hand to touch a long scratch down the side of his cheek.

Despite his appearance, his eyes were lit with humour, but he had not risen to greet her. He lay with one muscular arm bent to cradle his head. "What would Vigor say if he heard you tiptoing about the barn, calling for my Lord Harleston?" he asked, still amused.

"I doubt very much he could hear me," Susan answered, not willing to let him divert her attention. "But you must tell me what happened! I have been so worried, but I never thought you would come back like this! Did you have another accident?"

"Nothing so romantic, I'm afraid," he said, smothering a yawn. He seemed immeasurably weary, but his eyes glistened. "It was simply quite a task to lift that carriage. It must have been made entirely of iron. No wonder it has lasted so long."

Susan's big eyes grew wider in horror. "Don't tell me you righted it yourself!"

"All right, I won't tell you," said his lordship obligingly. "But I will tell you, I found no one else to do it. The locals became grossly occupied when I asked them for help. They must have sensed its weight by some look on my face. I had thought myself better at dissimulation."

"But couldn't you have paid them more? Surely someone would have done it, and I would gladly have paid you back with my father's money."

Lord Harleston hid a smile and looked at her sheepishly. "I forgot to replenish my purse," he admitted.

"You forgot to...?" Susan was speechless with dismay.

He nodded wearily, but still managed to see the humour in the situation. "When I finally got the carriage righted and started back in this direction, I had the devil's own time finding my way back. I see now why the people of this region were unaware of the Norman Conquest until twenty years after the Battle of Hastings—in spite of its being a mere thirty miles away. Most of them don't know their way as far as the next village, much less to London. I shouldn't wonder if they had not heard of it yet."

"Oh, you poor man!" wailed Susan, covering her face with her hands. "Oh, my lord, I am so sorry. I ought never to have mixed you up in my affairs."

"You had nothing to do with it," he reminded her. "I promised your father. Besides, if I don't regret it, even after the past two days—or is it three—why should you?"

"But this last is all my fault," Susan protested. "Your promise was to get me back into England, not to go running about the country on wild-goose chases. I gave you no choice in the matter when I offered to help Lady Mewhinny. But I never knew it would come to this! I beg your forgiveness, my lord. And tomorrow, when you have rested, we shall be off, and there will be no more of this groom nonsense!''

Tom lifted an offended eyebrow. "Am I to be turned off then, without proper notice? Is this how you thank a loyal servant?''

Susan would not be amused. She shook her head and refused to be teased out of her ill humour with herself.

Tom gave up his efforts with a weary sigh and closed his eyes. Then he said, ''I beg leave to remind you, madam, that my promise was to your father. I shall consider it discharged when, and only when, I have delivered you to complete safety. Let us have no more discussion on the matter. But tell me,'' he added, ''how have you got along? Did you find it difficult?''

"Oh, no,'' Susan said apologetically. "I have been most comfortable. It is so mortifying! I wish I could have changed places with you. Lady Mewhinny is a darling. She wants me to call her Kitty. And she keeps monkeys here, hundreds of them. It's a charity of hers.''

Lord Harleston's tired brain scarcely followed her disjointed speech, but he was relieved to see she had not been in danger. She was not to know it was worry for her which had caused him to hurry as much as he did, so that he forgot to refill his purse.

"I'm glad you were comfortable'' was all he said, closing his eyes.

"Oh, I was. I will admit the monkeys were a bit disconcerting at first. But Lady Mewhinny is so kind-hearted," she continued musing. "She treats them like pampered children. I only wonder what will happen to them when she's gone. It's not the kind of thing someone else is likely to be willing to do. Do you agree?"

Susan looked down to find his lordship's eyes firmly closed, but he managed to answer her with a mumble. "Quite mad." Her heart filled with remorse when she realized her concern for the monkeys had distracted her from his condition.

"But I was so worried about you," she said. "I could only think of the terrible inconvenience I had caused you—so unsuitable to your station. But if I had known what really was happening, I should have died of mortification."

He smiled sleepily. "Would you? Don't give it another thought. My only concern was for your safety."

Susan blushed and then wondered if he had really meant what he said, for he was suddenly asleep. The poor darling man, she thought, feeling so deeply for him she could almost sense the weariness in his limbs. She whispered his name once and then again, but he did not answer. Only then did she put out a hand to touch his cheek. His boyish blond hair was caked with mud, but still shone in the light of the lanterns. She brushed a lock of it away from his scratch and winced at the sight of it.

Looking around the stable, she saw a bucket of water and some pieces of cloth. Though rough, at least they were clean. She dipped one in the water and brought it back to wash the mud from his face, hesitantly at first, but soon she saw nothing would wake him. When his worst scratches had been cleansed of dirt, Susan went on another search and found some horse blankets. They were coarse and terribly heavy, but they would keep him warm. The night air was cold and she feared his getting a chill after such exhaustion.

When his lordship was thoroughly covered and tucked round with the blankets, she rose and reluctantly prepared to leave. Looking down at him one last time, Susan felt a pang of guilt mixed with overwhelming gratitude. Never had anyone exerted himself for her as Lord Harleston had done these past few days. She reminded herself how great his debt must have been to her father for him to engage in such a burdensome task as getting her back into England had proved to be. Loath to leave him alone in the great, empty room, she stooped once more and smoothed the hair away from his face. Her touch was gentle, but she discovered her hand was trembling and pulled it slowly away. With a deep sigh, she rose and made her way back to the house.

Once inside, Susan left instructions that Tom was not to be disturbed in the morning and sent a message to Lady Mewhinny indicating her intention to set out only when he should be rested and well fed. But she half expected to be told that Tom was up and ready to go by breakfast time, for she was certain Lord Harleston would wish to be on his way.

No MESSAGE to that effect came, however, and Susan went down to a late breakfast in time to catch Lady Mewhinny at her morning work.

"Are you staying on then, dear?" asked the kindly old lady. "I did so hope you would change your mind."

"S'ank you, Kitty, *non*. I cannot. It was just zat Tom was so exhausted I s'ought it best not to rush 'im zis morning."

"That is very thoughtful of you, Susan. And wise. You would not benefit from his coming down with something. Although I must say you surprise me—I had thought him stronger than Vigor. But perhaps I was wrong to send him."

Susan smothered a quick smile with a dainty cough. "It is perfectly all right, Kitty. I am certain zere was no 'arm done. But per'aps 'e *is* a slight bit weaker zan Vigor."

Lady Mewhinny nodded in agreement and went back to her work. Susan was touched by her attachment to her faithful old servant, which apparently kept her from seeing how ancient he had become. There must be something in the attitude, however, she had to admit, for Lady Mewhinny herself carried on as if fifty years more or less meant nothing to her own abilities.

By afternoon, Susan had begun to worry that all was not well with Tom, for she received no message from him at all. She had by now realized that he must not have slept for the past two days, perhaps more, but so prolonged a sleep could not be healthy, either. She was sitting with Lady Mewhinny in the drawing room before dinner when, at last, Bates brought the grim tidings.

"Pardon me, madam," he said with a slight bow, ignoring the eager expression on her face. "But I fear I must inform you of a slight impediment to your travelling plans."

Her face fell instantly and she swallowed, unable to speak. Turning, she silently sought Lady Mewhinny's help.

"What is it, Bates?" asked her ladyship calmly.

"It is madam's manservant, my lady. It would appear he has come down with a fever."

"Tom?" Susan said anxiously. "Tom is sick?"

"Quite, madam," confirmed Bates.

Susan rose to her feet immediately and put down her needlework. "I must see him," she said.

Lady Mewhinny looked at her in astonishment, "Go see him now, my dear? But you might catch something from him. Surely someone can see to it for you that he receives the proper attention."

Bates spoke in agreement, "Madam's maidservant is doing so at this very moment, my lady."

Susan's blood rose within her. Peg! "I am afraid not, Lady Mewhinny," she said, the effect of Bates's formality rubbing off on her. "I fear I must go myself." Then, as it was evident her hostess was about to protest again, Susan fell back upon her imaginary spouse. "You see, my 'usband, Mr. Faringdon, was quite fond of Tom. 'E was 'is most valued servant and 'is family 'as been attached to ze Faringdon estates for many generations. My conscience would not allow me to leave 'im entirely to strangers' 'ands. It would 'ave grieved my 'usband for me to do so."

This appeal sufficed and Lady Mewhinny conceded immediately. "Then you must go right ahead and see to it, my dear. And may I say how right you are to feel so. Too often, I fear, these old and valued loyalties are not attended to, to the detriment of country society. But do not tarry. I shall hold dinner for you."

Susan thanked her and did her best to leave the room without showing her extreme anxiety. Lord Harleston sick! And because of her. What if he should die?

But the sight which met her eyes as she strode into the stable was enough to banish that worry from her mind. Peg, that incorrigible flirt, was hovering over a prostrate Tom, bathing his chest with water from a bucket and giggling in his ears. He was stripped to the waist, at least, for not a speck of clothing covered him above the blanket, and Susan was not surprised to learn later just how thorough Peg had been.

"Peg!" she cried out, doing her best to control her anger. "What is ze meaning of zis? Why did you not tell me Tom was sick?"

The stupid girl turned and, seeing Susan, pouted before answering sulkily. "I didn't think you would want ter be bothered, miss," she said mendaciously. "I found 'im like this this mornin', all 'ot and fever-ish like. Poor cove!" she added with a smile for Tom's benefit.

"Peg has been taking good care of me, madam," said Tom hoarsely. He was glistening with sweat and Susan's anger left her as she saw the haze in his eyes. She had noticed it the night before and mistaken it for weariness. Now as she put her hand to his forehead, she was shocked to discover how hot he was.

But Lord Harleston had not entirely lost his sense of humour. "She has really been *most attentive*, madam," he added, a glint in his eye.

"I do not doubt it," said Susan dryly. "Zat was very good of you, Peg. Now, please take Tom's cloz'es into ze house and wash zem yourself. I do not want to inconvenience Lady Mewhinny's 'ousehold any more zan we shall 'ave to. It appears we shall be staying on anoz'er few days until Tom is well."

"I'll 'ave 'im up in no time," said Peg with a sly wink for Tom.

Susan swallowed a retort and said through tight-ened lips, "Please do as I said, Peg. And do 'ave someone tell Lady Mewhinny I shall not be up to din-ner. I can 'ave a tray later in my room."

"Oll right, miss," said Peg reluctantly. Then she took herself off with a toss of the head.

As soon as she was gone, Lord Harleston closed his eyes with relief and a shudder went through him. Susan's heart was wrenched with pity and her inhibitions melted away. "Oh, Tom!" she said remorsefully, forgetting for once to address him properly. "This is so horrible, and it is all my fault."

"Nonsense!" he said between chattering teeth. She drew the blanket up more closely around him and was glad to see Peg had found something more suitable than the horse blankets she had covered him with the night before. "It's just a chill," he said. "Had much worse in the Peninsula."

"But you poor, poor dear!"

Tom smiled and managed to cock an eye toward her. "I'm just grateful you saved me from Peg," he muttered. Susan looked at him suspiciously as his eyelids drooped again. He seemed to enjoy reminding her of Peg. She wondered if her annoyance were so obvious.

"I will see to it that you are well cared for, Lord Harleston," she said, affecting to ignore his last remark. "Lady Mewhinny will be happy to tell one of her servants to nurse you and I shall look in on you every day." Then she added under her breath, "And I shall make sure Peg does not disturb you." She sat silently awhile, allowing him to rest. Peg was certainly a problem; she must keep her busy somehow in the house. The girl had not come to offer her services in the past two days, and Susan had not bothered to call her. She had been much happier forgetting about Peg entirely, but that must change. The girl wanted watching.

"Captain," his lordship mumbled, rousing her suddenly from her thoughts. Surprised, Susan looked down and saw a frown on his face. "Captain!" he shouted clearly.

"Lord Harleston," she whispered emphatically. "You must keep your voice down. What is it you wish to say about my father?"

"Save me from Peg, Captain!" For a moment, Susan thought he was just teasing her, but gradually she realized he had become delirious. The knowledge frightened her. She quickly put her hand to his head again and felt how much hotter he had become in just the past few minutes. The fever was raging and she had to do something about it.

Picking up the rag Peg had used, she began to bathe his arms and face, hardly thinking of what she was doing. Harleston continued to mumble, and she caught her father's name several times. The captain was clearly on his mind and he was worried about something. She tried to talk to him and reassure him that all was well as she prayed the warm water would cool his fever.

After a while, her efforts seemed to calm him and he stopped his raving. With relief she put down her bathing cloth and regarded him for a moment. Only then did she become aware of the beauty of his figure as he lay there in the straw. Peg had given him a thorough washing. It was plain to see, for he had none of the layer of dirt she had seen on him the night before. But it would not have mattered anyway, she admitted, as her eyes looked him over tenderly, for he was magnificent either way. She reached a gentle hand up to his hair and removed a lock from his dampened forehead.

"Oh, Tom," she whispered hopelessly.

"I done the washin', miss, like you arst me," said Peg at her elbow.

Susan jumped and retracted her hand. "Zat is excellent, Peg," she said hastily. "I was just feeling Tom's fore'ead to see if 'is fever was down, but it is much worse. I am afraid I shall 'ave to nurse 'im myself."

"But, miss!" Peg protested, clearly disappointed. "You can't do that! I'll make sure 'e gets wot's needed," she added innocently.

"Zat is very selfless of you, Peg," said Susan ironically, "but I shall need you to carry water for me, and to wash ze cloz'es and linens. And besides, Lady Mewhinny will be grateful for your 'elp in ze 'ouse. We 'ave been a dreadful charge upon 'er."

"But that's not fair," whined Peg, now mindless of her noble pose.

"That will be all, Peg!" Susan said dreadfully. "Now, run back into ze 'ouse and fetch me more pieces of linen." Then as Peg seemed about to refuse to budge, Susan marshalled every ounce of strength within her to say firmly, "Go!"

The girl flounced out of the stable without so much as an "Oll right, miss." Susan watched her go with a sigh of despair. *Wretched creature,* she thought. Peg had a sensuality so extreme that it amounted to a sixth sense. She seemed to have sensed intuitively, without consciousness, that Susan was still a maiden, for no amount of prompting or correction could make her address her mistress as madam.

Banishing Peg from her mind with a will, Susan turned back to attend to his lordship.

"I shall have to nurse you," she explained to him quietly, "or you shall give us all away." His mutterings centred so frequently on Captain Johnstone that it worried her. She wondered what could be troubling him about her father, never realizing that it was *she* who was on his mind, that during his ordeal of the past two days, he had greatly feared leaving her to carry on alone.

Peg brought the linens and departed again in silent sulks. Susan did not allow that to disturb her, but she was less composed when she picked up one of the pieces of cloth to bathe Tom down. This time, she could not avoid the feeling that she was taking liberties with his person. It was impossible to keep separate in her mind the acts of nursing him and the notion of a caress. In fact, she was so overcome with sudden shyness that she had to talk to herself firmly before she could carry on.

"You did the same thing for your father, didn't you?" she said, dipping the linen in the water and wringing it out mercilessly. Still, she found herself staring at him wonderingly from time to time, appreciating the firmness of his muscles and the grace in his neck and hands. It was not until he started tossing again, that she managed to forget her feelings for a moment and apply herself to soothing him. In the end, though, things got worse, for her ministrations were so effective that Tom began to smile and mutter softly in his sleep.

An overwhelming curiosity to know what he was dreaming about got the better of her, and as Susan bent her ear down closer to his lips, Lord Harleston groaned and flung his arm across her, turning her over and pinning her against the stable floor. She shrieked, shocked into emitting a louder noise than she should have. Then, after struggling futilely for a moment against the burden of his bare chest, she stopped momentarily to catch her breath and took time to think.

Perhaps I should not disturb him, she thought tenderly, rather enjoying the feel of his arm across her. She stole a hand up and stroked the back of his head, taking pleasure in the feel of his smooth, fine locks. But no sooner had she given herself up to the quite tolerable prospect of staying there until he rolled himself over again, than Lord Harleston ruined it with a clearly uttered word.

"Maria," he groaned on a lingering note.

Susan's hand froze in midstroke. Her chest rose mightily in spite of the dead weight upon it. "Maria!" she declared with no little indignation. Lord

Harleston did not respond. He was obviously in the grip of some pleasant dream.

A surge of unexpected strength filled Susan and with both arms she heaved his body clear of her own, mumbling angrily, "Move over, you great hulking oaf."

His lordship rolled onto his back with another groan of "Captain." Susan sat up and began to brush the hay from her dress and hair, but the sound of a familiar voice raised in shock brought her to her feet instantly.

"Susan! My dear!" cried Lady Mewhinny. "Whatever are you doing?"

Susan turned to find her hostess standing at the entrance to the stall. Her mouth flew open wordlessly. Then she swallowed as the colour leapt to her cheeks.

"Lady Mewhinny!" she cried faintly. "I was just ... zat is, I was ... I was trying to turn 'im," she finished. "'E 'as a considerable fever and I was trying to cool 'im down."

Lady Mewhinny approached poor Tom with a lantern held high above her head. "But you weren't going to care for him yourself, my dear?" she asked in a tone of mild reproach.

"Yes, I must," said Susan, deeply embarrassed nonetheless. "You see, in France, we always nurse our own servants. I would not feel right allowing someone else to do it. It is my charitable duty."

"Oh, dear," said Lady Mewhinny, distressed, but accepting. "You do have some rather uncomfortable national customs, do you not? I suppose I should feel a similar responsibility should Vigor ever fall ill. But he never does, of course. But, my dear, you cannot do everything for Tom. He is much too heavy for you to lift."

"Zat he is," agreed Susan feelingly, and she blushed. "But I can call someone for assistance when I need it. Peg removed 'is cloz'ing," she added, in case there were some doubt.

"Yes, you must," agreed her ladyship, apparently ignoring her last remark. "You must call Vigor. But I would not use your maidservant; she can help my staff with the monkeys while Vigor is helping you." Lady Mewhinny's eyes held an enigmatic look.

"Vigor will be much better," Susan agreed. "And per'aps 'e could sleep 'ere beside Tom in case 'e needs anys'ing during ze night."

"I shall see to it immediately," said Lady Mewhinny briskly. She had an air about her which said that everything was now arranged. "I shall have your supper sent to your room, dear. Shall we say in half an hour?"

Susan thanked her and said she would be along directly.

As soon as Lady Mewhinny's tiny form had passed through the stable doors, Susan returned her attention to Tom. He had flung both arms outside the covers and she could see that he was shivering.

"Oh, dear!" Susan cried, immediately forgetting her anger of moments before. She knelt and covered

him up again, tucking the blankets tightly around him
and hoping he would not kick them off in the night.
It was true she would not be able to watch him round
the clock. Even could she have done it, it would have
appeared much too strange for her to devote herself so
entirely to a groom. Lady Mewhinny's suggestion of
Vigor had come at just the right time, for Susan,
thinking quickly, had remembered how hard of hearing he was. If Tom—Lord Harleston—should utter
any words to give them away, she thought, Vigor
would likely not hear them.

Lord Harleston muttered something and tried to roll
again in his sleep. Her heart pounding within her, Susan knelt closer to hear. This time, she placed both
hands upon his chest to make certain there would be
no repetition of the last incident.

"Yes, Tom, what is it?" she whispered gently,
straining to hear. He mumbled again faintly and she
sighed with disappointment. It was all so indistinct.

Then he spoke again quite clearly. "Susan," he said,
a little smile playing about his lips. And then, "So
beautiful."

Susan's heart melted within her and tears came to
her eyes. "Oh, Tom," she whispered again, moving
her hand gently over his feverish lips. She let it linger
there for a moment before pulling it back into her lap.
It was such a temptation to kiss him as he lay there
helpless in the straw.

You must get a grip on yourself, Susan told herself,
sighing. She must not let Lord Harleston's helpless

state trick her into fancying herself in love with him. She was not completely unaware of her own weaknesses. But as she gazed down at him and watched the play of lantern light across his strongly cut features, a wealth of tenderness rose up inside her. It was somehow different, and more than all the passions that had been aroused in her over the years; more than her concern for Lady Mewhinny; more, even, than her love for her father those last few weeks.

Suddenly, the strength of these feelings frightened her. She had allowed herself to develop an attachment that must not be. Had she not known from the beginning that Lord Harleston must not be involved in her escapade? Was she falling in love? Susan steeled herself against such a notion. As soon as Tom was well, she would insist upon his leaving her to her own devices. With what was left of her father's fifty pounds she could easily make the rest of the journey by post. No one would be likely to discover her, and his lordship could have no qualms.

She sighed again and rose to her feet as Vigor entered the stables. A glance at his bent and feeble frame sent a feeling of remorse through her as she realized the chore to which she had set him.

"Are you certain you will be all right out here, Vigor?" she asked him.

"Beg pardon, miss?" he said, one hand cupped to his ear.

Susan spoke a little louder, "I was asking if you would be quite comfortable!"

"Oh, we'll make him comfortable, miss. Never you worry," said the old groom. He began to set out the blankets for his own makeshift bed in the stall next to Tom's as if it were something he did quite often.

Susan watched him with resignation and then left the stable as he bade her good-night. She hoped Tom would be better by morning.

CHAPTER SEVEN

BUT TOM WAS STILL very feverish the next day and showed no signs of awareness. With Vigor's help, Susan managed to get a little broth down his throat, and some water, but she wondered if she should ask Lady Mewhinny to send for a doctor. Only the thought that Lord Harleston might give them away kept her from making the request, not because she feared for her own safety, but because of the danger to his lordship's reputation were his complicity discovered.

By nightfall, she was at least satisfied that his fever was down and she left him to Vigor hoping for the best and giving instructions that she should be called if Tom took a turn for the worse.

The next morning when she arrived in the stables, Vigor had left his post, but not before filling the bucket with warm water. Susan felt his lordship's forehead and was considerably relieved to feel a lessening of his temperature. He slept on, however, and she applied herself to the task of removing his perspiration from the night before.

After dipping a fresh piece of linen into the water and wringing it thoroughly, she first bathed Lord Harleston's face, smoothing his fine hair back with a gentle hand. Then she freshened her cloth and began bathing his neck and torso. His skin was smooth and hairless on the inner portion of his arms, showing the highly developed muscles and veins in great detail. His firm chest also was relatively free of hair except for a soft covering of a pale, almost reddish colour. Susan had just begun to bathe him gently, smiling and crooning unconsciously to herself, when her hand froze in sudden dismay.

She experienced a cold, prickly feeling as if someone were watching her and, looking up, saw Lord Harleston's brown eyes gleaming at her in a most disconcerting fashion. Slowly she withdrew her hand from his chest with as much dignity as she could muster.

"Lord Harleston," she said in a curiously trembling voice. She had hoped to sound cheerful, but distantly cool as a nurse should. She cleared her throat and tried again. "You are better." She could feel the surge of colour flooding her from head to toe.

A smile played about the corners of his mouth. "Yes. *Most* comfortable." He raised himself up on one elbow, still looking at her with that fixed gleam in his eye.

"You have been quite feverish," she said quickly. "It was most alarming. I was just...bathing you down to lower the fever."

Drat the man, Susan thought. He still refused to help her out of her confusion. "*Thank* you" was all he said, and in an odiously insinuating way.

NO COST! NO OBLIGATION TO BUY! NO PURCHASE NECESSARY!

PLAY "LUCKY 7"
AND GET AS MANY AS SIX FREE GIFTS . . .

HOW TO PLAY:

1. With a coin, carefully scratch off the silver box at the right. This makes you eligible to receive one or more free books, and possibly other gifts, depending on what is revealed beneath the scratch-off area.

2. You'll receive brand-new Harlequin Regency™ novels. When you return this card, we'll send you the books and gifts you qualify for *absolutely free!*

3. If we don't hear from you, every other month we'll send you 4 additional novels to read and enjoy. You can return them and owe nothing but if you decide to keep them, you'll pay only $2.49* per book, a savings of 26¢ each off the cover price! There is *no* extra charge for postage and handling. There are no hidden extras.

4. When you join the Harlequin Reader Service®, you'll get our members' only newsletter, as well as additional free gifts from time to time just for being a member.

5. You must be completely satisfied. You may cancel at any time simply by sending us a note or a shipping statement marked "cancel" or returning any unopened shipment to us at our cost.

You'll love your elegant 20k gold electroplated chain! The necklace is finely crafted with 160 double-soldered links and is electroplate finished in genuine 20k gold. And it's yours free as added thanks for giving our Reader Service a try!

PLAY "LUCKY 7"

Just scratch off the silver box with a coin.
Then check below to see which gifts you get.

YES! I have scratched off the silver box. Please send me all the gifts for which I qualify. I understand I am under no obligation to purchase any books, as explained on the opposite page.

(U-H-RG-04/90)
248 CIH 4AJK

NAME

ADDRESS   APT

CITY   STATE   ZIP

7	7	7	WORTH FOUR FREE BOOKS, FREE GOLD ELECTROPLATED CHAIN AND MYSTERY BONUS
🍒	🍒	🍒	WORTH FOUR FREE BOOKS AND MYSTERY BONUS
●	●	●	WORTH FOUR FREE BOOKS
🔔	🔔	🍒	WORTH TWO FREE BOOKS

HARLEQUIN "NO RISK" GUARANTEE
• You're not required to buy a single book—ever!
• You must be completely satisfied or you may cancel at any time simply by sending us a note or a shipping statement marked "cancel" or by returning any unopened shipment to us at our cost. Either way, you will receive no more books; you'll have no further obligation.
• The free books and gifts you receive from this "Lucky 7" offer remain yours to keep no matter what you decide.

If offer card is missing, write to:
Harlequin Reader Service, 901 Fuhrmann Blvd., P.O. Box 1867, Buffalo, N.Y. 14269-1867

Susan felt her temper rising. After all the trouble she had been to, it was quite unfair of him to tease her. "I *had* to nurse you myself," she said with asperity. "You were delirious and kept calling out my father's name. I was afraid you would give us both away." Susan did not say her real concern had been for him, but she was relieved to see a quick frown replace his teasing smile.

Lord Harleston rose to a sitting position and ran his hands through his tousled hair. "I am sorry," he said. "I cannot think what happened, but I really am quite grateful for all your bother."

Susan ignored the last part of his speech and seized upon a safer topic. "Well, *I* certainly can. You had no sleep for upwards of three days and then set out in the cold to do the work of a Titan. We shall not go on until you have had a chance to recover your strength. Lady Mewhinny is very kind and will not at all mind our staying until you are better.

"I can only wonder what possessed you to perform such a task," she added. "You ought to have gone on to London and left me here. I could have done very well on my own."

Tom gave her a quizzing look. "Well, first I might remind you of my pledge to your father. But I rather think I have you to blame for it."

"Me?" Susan wished she could sound more outraged, but the truth was she agreed with him.

He nodded. "I seem to have caught a bad habit from you. I have the most irrational need to rush about saving people from calamities. Never had it before. It must be catching."

Susan flushed and he grinned at her discomfort. She decided not to respond to his sally, but instead asked, "How are you feeling this morning?"

"I am quite better now, thank you. But another day of rest does not sound a bad idea. Where are my clothes?" he asked suddenly, looking about him and noticing his state of undress.

"I shall have them brought to you directly," said Susan, trying to act as though there were nothing disturbing about his present state. "Peg removed them," she added pointedly.

Lord Harleston smiled wickedly. "I seem to remember that."

"I shall have Vigor return them," said Susan, rising to her feet and ignoring the provocation. "He stayed with you here at night and was most helpful in lifting you to be fed. Though you must be famished, for all we got down you was a few sips of broth. You seemed quite anxious to be protected from Peg, by the way—crying out for help, and carrying on."

She was amused to see that Lord Harleston finally had the grace to blush. He quickly reached up a hand and took hers before she could depart.

"My dear Mrs. Faringdon," he said in a strangely serious voice. "Pray accept my thanks."

Susan's eyes met his and then faltered. "It was nothing," she said. "Nothing compared to what you have risked for me. It is I who should be thanking you.''

Seeing her extreme confusion, he kissed her hand lightly and released it, saying, ''Thanks accepted. Now, I would be most grateful for my clothes and a bit of breakfast.''

Promising to see to it right away, Susan left him with a glowing heart. The sight of Tom well and in full humour had filled her with a bubbling sense of happiness. Not until she had seen him thus had she realized how much she had missed his teasing company. And there had been something about that look in his eye which, although disturbing, had elated her beyond measure. In it there had been amusement, yes, but also pleasure, and desire.

Susan left orders with Bates to see that Tom's clothes should be brought to him and a hearty meal sent to build back his strength. If the elderly butler found anything strange in her constant attention to the welfare of her groom, he gave no indication, but bowed politely and said it should be done. Then Susan went in search of Lady Mewhinny.

She found the diminutive lady engaged in supervising the scrubbing of the cages. The nervous animals were so excited with this activity, despite its familiarity, that they had set themselves to shrieking at an unbelievable pitch. The noise did not seem to disturb their mistress, however, for she listened calmly to Susan's shouts with one ear while directing the operation from a chair.

"I am so glad he is better, my dear," she said, managing to make herself heard above the din with little effort. "I was afraid you would worry too much about him. Vigor could have seen you safely home, you know, but I did not care to suggest it. Tom seems a truly faithful servant."

Susan smiled to herself and agreed. "Indeed 'e is, Kitty, and I 'ad to reward 'is loyalty wiz my attention. If you would not mind too much, in fact, I should like to stay on a day or two until 'e is more definitely well. Per'aps I could 'elp you wiz ze monkeys," she added, thinking she ought now to appear less interested in her groom.

The suggestion delighted Lady Mewhinny, so Susan stayed with her most of the day, resisting the temptation to check on Tom that night. It would appear all too strange, she thought, to continue to give him attention when he was well able to care for himself. The next day she exhibited similar restraint, only waiting for the afternoon when she would go down with his "instructions" for their departure the following day.

AFTER A DAY AND A HALF of food and rest, Tom was quite himself and anxious to start their journey. It was high time they stopped this masquerade, he thought. Surely they would find some other way to travel which would not make it so impossible for them to speak freely. He was whistling to himself as he brushed down the horses, hoping for a chance to speak with Susan later in the day, when a female voice greeted him from the door of the stables. He whirled round happily, only to find Peg approaching him with a seductive look in her eye.

"Hallo, Peg," he greeted her cheerfully, bracing himself for the onslaught.

"I 'eard you were up and about again," said Peg coyly. "An' I can see you're lookin' chipper. Thought y'might like to 'ave a little visit."

"Thanks, Peg. But I'm not quite up to snuff," he demurred. "Still a little weak, if you know what I mean. That fever really knocked me up."

"Oh, I don't know about that," said Peg, letting her eyes run up and down his figure suggestively. "You look ready for anything, I'd say."

Lord Harleston experienced a feeling of alarm. Drat the wench! Was she going to make him blush?

He turned back to his work anxiously. "Good of you to come, Peg. But I wouldn't want to get you in trouble with Mrs. Faringdon. She's got the devil of a temper, you know."

The gambit did not work. Peg came close beside the horse he was brushing and sat down, nearly reclining at his feet in the straw. He tried to avoid watching her as he worked, but had an irrational fear that she might spring on him if he didn't.

"Don't I know it," the girl agreed. "Liked to scratch my eyes out, she did, for puttin' you to bed the way I did. As if there was somethin' wrong with it and any decent, kind-'earted soul wouldn'a done the same thing.'' She glanced up at him from under her eye-lashes as if hoping to awaken a memory.

"Did she now?" he asked, ignoring it. "Was she so angry as to give you a hard time?"

"I'll say she was. Made me do the wash and 'elp with them blood—them monkeys,'' she corrected herself. "Wanted to nurse you 'erself, she did. Thought she might fancy a bit of a go with you 'er-self.'' She smiled provocatively as though she had paid him a compliment.

Lord Harleston gritted his teeth in sudden irrita-tion. "Don't speak of the mistress that way, Peg,'' he said seriously. Then he added lamely, "She might hear you."

"Oll right," said Peg, unconcernedly. "I *will* give 'er one thing. She's just that smart.''

"Oh?"

"Yeah. Fancy 'er learnin' English as fast as she done. An' 'er not speakin' above ten words when she first took me on.''

Lord Harleston smiled quietly to himself. So Susan had tired of playing her part. He did not worry, though, for obviously Peg, in spite of noticing a dif-ference, had no suspicion of there being another rea-son for it. Lady Mewhinny, by all rights, must be mad as a hatter and extremely frail to boot, as he recalled from the one time he'd seen her. It was hardly likely she would be so alert as to spot a fraud.

"Oh, smart she is," he agreed, happy to have found his excuse. "And she watches me like a hawk. I'm always worried about losing my place if she catches me out. And you had better be off now, too. I wouldn't want you to be turned off either.''

Peg rose reluctantly to her feet and moved closer. ''Oh, I'll prob'ly find meself another spot in Lunnon when we gets there,'' she said saucily. ''But not before you're feelin' a might stronger, I 'ope.'' She edged herself between Tom and his horse and gazed up at him invitingly. His lordship was looking down at her, biting his lip and trying to think his way out of this spot, when a sudden sound behind him signalled his relief.

''Peg!'' cried Susan sharply. The unrepentant girl sighed her disappointment and turned to greet her mistress. Susan stood with arms folded in a gesture of displeased authority. Peg bobbed a curtsey and said, ''Yes, miss,'' as though she'd been interrupted in her duties.

''Go into ze 'ouse at once and see to your chores, you lazy girl. I will not 'ave you wasting Tom's time out 'ere in ze stables. We will be leaving zis 'ouse tomorrow and I need you to pack.''

''Oll right, miss,'' said Peg, eyeing her sulkily and then turning to bestow a wink upon Tom. ''I won't be sorry to see the last of this place and them monkeys.'' She moved away slowly, not omitting to wiggle her hips and casting a glance back in Tom's direction before passing through the door.

After she had gone, Tom fell back against his horse and uttered a sigh of relief. "I thought you would never arrive."

"Um-hmmm," agreed Susan, tapping her fingers unconsciously against her forearm and still in her offended posture. "I daresay it is quite a trial for you."

"It is. Turrible," Lord Harleston teased. "And I cannot risk offending her, you know, for she would think it strange for me to be completely unresponsive."

"I see," said Susan. "Yes, I understand perfectly. That's why I put on such a show of anger, too, you know. It's all to convince her of my identity. It seems the genuine thing to do." Tom was nodding in agreement, and she was glad to see he looked slightly less sure of himself.

"Are you quite recovered now?" she asked, choosing to change the subject. "I suppose we ought to be leaving."

"Yes, I'm fine, thank you, and quite ready to go. I will have the carriage ready for you in the morning, madam," said Tom, with a bow and a tug at his forelock.

Susan could not resist the impish look he gave her and smiled playfully in return. "Thank you, Tom. Have the horses put to at six-thirty, please. I shall be at the door and ready by seven."

Lord Harleston bowed and then straightened, looking at her strangely. Susan fancied he was about to address her in seriousness when they both were distracted by the sound of wheels in the drive. A carriage was arriving.

"Ho!" came Vigor's quavery tones from outside the stable. "Tom! Give a hand here!"

Tom took Susan by the arm and pulled her out of sight of the door. "I will have to help him bring in the horses. Will I speak to you again this evening or must you go?"

Susan was suddenly shy. "I'm afraid I must go," she said, averting her eyes slightly from his intense gaze. Her fine black hair fell gently forward about her temples. "Dinner will be soon, and if this is to be my last evening here, I must be mindful of my duties to Lady Mewhinny. I shall be rather sad to leave her," she finished wistfully, "knowing I cannot ever come back to see her as myself. She must never know of my problems."

Lord Harleston frowned. He wanted to tell Susan of his plans to secure her pardon but was fearful of raising her hopes too soon. Surely the Prince would grant it. He could not allow her to be punished for an act of compassion! The thought sent a shot of fear through him, greater than any he had experienced in battle. Susan was refusing to meet his eye, but he could imagine the sadness in her expression. She had an open, impulsive nature, not intended for a life of concealment.

All at once, his lordship wondered how much it was for himself that he desired her pardon. But now there was no time for discussion. He let go of her arm at the sound of another cry from Vigor.

"I must go, too. But please do not worry. We shall see about everything."

He gave her an encouraging smile and hurried off to help the old groom. Susan, sighing, lifted her skirts and picked her way back to the house, being careful to stay out of sight of the new arrivals.

Inside, she found the servants in rather a perturbed state. It appeared that Lady Mewhinny's nephew, Mr. Augustus Petworthy, had come to stay unexpectedly, bringing with him a strange guest. From the rare, disgruntled expression on Bates's face, Susan guessed that Mr. Petworthy was not popular with the servants.

"Does he often arrive unannounced like this?" Susan enquired of the butler.

"Seldom unannounced, madam," said Bates, deigning for once to discuss matters. "Though never with more than a few days' notification. And he is not in the habit of bringing uninvited guests as if this were his own residence. Or likely to be," he added significantly.

"I see," said Susan, although she was not perfectly enlightened. She went upstairs to change into her black silk mourning gown for dinner. She had only two dresses to wear, not judging it correct for her to be out of mourning. Lady Mewhinny's dresser, another elderly servant named Simmons, had been keeping them fresh for her, but she was relieved there had been no other guests present during the few days of her stay. They might have thought it quite odd for a widow in such comfortable circumstances as to have her own carriage, to have no more than two mourning gowns to her name.

She went down to dinner just before six and was presented to Mr. Petworthy and his guest.

"Enchanté, madame," said Mr. Petworthy with a broad, tight-lipped smile which did not light his eyes. "I have heard the remarkable story of your assistance to my Aunt Catherine and may I say how truly grateful I am. I am quite devoted to her. Indeed, my friend here, Mr. Sodporth, will tell you how often I have spoken of her and in what affection I hold her." He turned and presented the gentleman at his side.

Susan could not truthfully say that she was favourably impressed with either gentleman. While there was nothing specifically in their manners to offend, there was something about them she could not quite like. Mr. Petworthy was a large man with a rather red face and round nose. His hair was cut "à la Brutus," but the back of his head was perfectly flat and he kept it always at a slight tilt which she found distracting. There was an alertness about him which suggested a need to be constantly seeking points of weakness in others and she later found his questions to be both probing and annoying.

Mr. Sodporth, who was introduced to her as a medical man, seemed to have very little to say for himself, but he clearly had a love of comfort. He was small and slightly nervous, so that whenever a remark was addressed to him, he bobbed his head up and down repeatedly with more than the necessary agreement. The rest of the time, he looked anxiously about him and awaited each delicacy placed before him with such anticipation that he seemed hardly aware of the conversation going on around the table. Lady Mewhinny's sherry, brandy and pastries were gobbled up in a state of total absorption.

Lady Mewhinny seemed to accept her visitors without the slightest bother or worry. She carried on quite as if her nephew were free to come and go as he chose. Susan had watched her during Mr. Petworthy's profession of devotion, but aside from looking up once from her needlework, Lady Mewhinny had shown no sign of being moved.

The dinner table conversation revolved largely around Mr. Sodporth's distinguished qualifications, although that gentleman showed more interest in his piece of mutton than in Mr. Petworthy's eloquent praise. According to him, Mr. Sodporth was an authority on the subject of melancholia and despondency. Lady Mewhinny listened brightly but without much comment, so Susan was obliged to appear more interested than she truly was. Mr. Petworthy seemed quite eager to impress them with his friend's accomplishments.

"But I daresay you have little knowledge of medical matters, Mrs. Faringdon," he said, turning to her finally. "It has just occurred to me to ask whether you are a part of the Hertfordshire branch of the Faring-don family. I am quite well acquainted with Sir Donald, but I do not recall his having mentioned the recent loss of a family member.''

Susan cringed inwardly, but lifted her head with dignity and replied in as crushing a tone as she could muster, ''*Non, monsieur.* We do not form part of zat branch of ze family.''

''What a pity,'' said Mr. Petworthy in heartfelt tones. Nevertheless, Susan got the distinct impression that he was relieved. ''Then we cannot be acquainted. Still, I shall mention our having met to Sir Donald next time I visit him. It will be sure to interest him. Now, tell me,'' he continued, tilting his big head round to face her and smiling in a way she found offensive, ''how much longer have we to look forward to the pleasure of your company?''

''I shall be leaving in ze morning, *monsieur,*'' she answered without showing her relief. With his arrival she had felt obliged to reapply herself to her French accent, although having had an English husband excused her from total ignorance of the English tongue.

He tuttutted with a cheery smile and turned back to solicit the attention of Lady Mewhinny.

''Auntie!'' he said rather loudly, as if he thought she were deaf. ''I must thank you for providing my friend and me with such a charming companion for the evening.'' He glanced back at Susan, giving her a look of complicity, and went on in a condescending aside, ''for you must know we are not usually so gay here.''

Then, fortunately, with this rather heavy-handed compliment he seemed to have finished with Mrs. Faringdon, for he ignored her for the rest of the evening.

"Auntie," he began again. "I will hope for a few minutes of your time after dinner to discuss a matter of business with you. I have come into the way of an extraordinary opportunity about which I could not conscionably omit telling you."

"That is very thoughtful of you, Augustus," said Lady Mewhinny complacently. "But as you know, my fortune is all in the funds."

"Of course, of course, Auntie," said Mr. Petworthy impatiently. "But you must let me tell you about my extreme good fortune in hearing of this investment. No matter how ably your man of business is handling your affairs, you could not possibly wish to refuse hearing of something which could treble your income. Just think of what it could mean to your monkeys," he added with a tight little smile.

"Why, Augustus!" cried her ladyship laughingly. "Have you at last developed an affection for my monkeys? I warned you it would happen if you continued to visit me. They are quite irresistable!"

Mr. Petworthy did not answer immediately, but gave the impression of swallowing a retort.

"You must know, my dear Susan," continued Lady Mewhinny, "that Augustus feels himself very ill-used by my monkeys and me, not to mention Sir William. I am afraid it was a grave shock to him when Sir William left his entire fortune to me. It was unentailed, you see. And I, of course, need the better part of it for my poor monkeys."

Susan felt the gentleman tense in his seat beside her, but he managed to address himself to his aunt with rigid composure. "Nonsense, Auntie," he said, smiling for Susan's benefit. "You are only joking. Why, my uncle made me such a generous allowance that I have nothing to wish for."

Mr. Sodporth looked up from his food at this statement as if it came as a surprise, but nodded and smiled dumbly when Mr. Petworthy gave him a shrivelling look.

"But I have to admit," said Mr. Petworthy to Susan with the appearance of one mildly aggrieved, "that it comes as rather a shock to a man of such strong family devotion as myself, to find that his only uncle—an uncle moreover with no other living descendants—that said uncle arranged his affairs in such an extraordinary manner. Is the claim of charity," he continued, "charity to mere animals, mind you, greater than the attachment of blood between generations? It leaves one with great questions and doubts—doubts that perhaps all was not quite well with his mind when he made his dispositions. Perhaps Mr. Sodporth would feel able to advance a theory to enlighten us on this matter."

Mr. Sodporth, thus called upon in the middle of a mouthful of boiled potatoes, gasped in surprise and immediately choked upon his food. Lady Mewhinny made a casual sign to an elderly footman, who approached the visitor and clapped him soundly on the back. The others went on with their conversation politely, as though the disturbance had not occurred.

"I sincerely doubt, Augustus," said Lady Mewhinny calmly, "that your concern for my monkeys has undergone an improvement. I should be happy to learn that you had experienced a change of heart, for I would be glad to have some assistance. As I have told you before, it astonishes me how anyone with a name such as yours can have so little regard for our more unfortunate species." She gave a little chuckle at her own joke and looked to Susan for her reaction.

The curious inappropriateness of Mr. Petworthy's name had already occurred to Susan, so she was able to smile at her hostess without offending the gentleman next to her with an extreme show of amusement. Mr. Petworthy had clearly been subjected to this humour before, for he made no attempt to offer a polite laugh. Instead, he applied himself to his food for the first time that evening, and the remainder of the meal passed in relative silence.

After dinner, however, he was sufficiently recovered to corner her ladyship as she was rising from the table, so Susan had to move into the parlour without her companionship. Lady Mewhinny promised to join her shortly, but the time stretched out slowly, so Susan decided to go up to her room to add some finishing touches to her packing. When she came back down and started to enter the parlour, she became aware of gentlemen's voices on the other side of the door. Not wanting to enter the room unless she was certain of Lady Mewhinny's protective presence, she waited and listened with the object of detecting her voice.

But in a moment it became quite clear that her ladyship could not possibly be present. While Susan listened in increasing distress, Mr. Petworthy expressed his loathing for his aunt in the most shockingly disrespectful terms.

"The old witch!" came his voice from the parlour. "Petworthy, indeed! I shall see to it that those miserable apes are tossed out as soon as she is gone. You were no help to me tonight, Alfred. You and your appetite. You might strive to look as though you occasionally experienced a decent meal, instead of slobbering over every dish that comes round. I am certain *I*, at least, have fed you often enough."

"I was only being polite, Augustus. You never said I was not to enjoy myself. I am quite prepared to be of service to you when the time comes," responded Mr. Sodporth in an injured tone.

"Well, never mind that. It's a good thing that Frenchwoman plans to leave in the morning. It might be harder for us to do what we have to if she were around. And I cannot hold off my creditors much longer. Once she is gone we can get to work in earnest."

"The old lady did not tumble to your investment scheme?" asked his accomplice.

"No," answered Mr. Petworthy shortly. "She's got a solicitor who handles all her affairs. Not a day under eighty, I imagine, but she always prefers his judgement to mine. There's absolutely no accounting for it," he added with a peculiar ingenuousness.

Susan wanted to listen more to see if she could find out their intentions, but the two men made sounds as if they might leave the parlour, so she fled quickly up the stairs and went straight to her room.

CHAPTER EIGHT

ONCE INSIDE IT, Susan collapsed against the closed door in horror. Mr. Petworthy's intentions with respect to his aunt were evil ones, she was certain. No lighter interpretation could possibly be made of his comments. He was desperate for funds, and he and the doctor had come down into Sussex with an idea for disposing somehow of poor Kitty! She must do something fast, but yet she had no information on which to act.

What was it he had said? Oh, yes, she recalled: he was happy that she should be leaving in the morning for that would make his task easier. Then I must not leave, thought Susan anxiously. How could she, when Lady Mewhinny needed her so desperately? She, of course, would be unaware of her nephew's evil intent, and perhaps would not even believe it if Susan were to tell her.

Then Tom and I must handle it, Susan decided. Yet how were they to make an excuse in order to stay on when she had clearly said they would leave on the morrow? She must get a message to Tom so that he could make up an excuse—a broken carriage wheel or some such thing. He would know what to do.

It was then that it occurred to her she must not assume Lord Harleston would be game to stay on at her
bidding. "Oh, I've already involved you in enough of
my nonsense," she said miserably, as though he were
there in the room with her. "I must not drag you into
this." There was nothing for it but to explain the situation to Lord Harleston and ask him to leave. She
would have to stay on with Lady Mewhinny alone.
Knowing him as she now did, she was certain he would
put up a fuss, but she must convince him somehow.
The clandestine nature of their friendship posed its
own dangers, chiefly to her heart. Had she not just
started planning his involvement again? It seemed so
easy to forget who he really was and why they were
there. He was much too reliable, too comforting and
too strong. If he continued to help her, she would not
be able to stop her feelings for him from developing.
So he must, he absolutely must, go this time.

It was a painful decision, but once having made it,
Susan did not hesitate for an instant. She would have
to be certain of the message getting to him, she realized, for there was no time for mistakes. Hastily taking a pen and some paper from the elaborately gilded
escritoire in her chamber, she wrote a careful message
in French so that none of the servants would be able
to read it.

"Come to my room at midnight," she wrote. She
started to add, "I must speak to you urgently," but
was not certain of some of the French words. So after
struggling over it for what seemed a considerable waste

of time, she decided a person as intelligent as Lord Harleston would certainly know she had urgent need of him, and the phrase would not be necessary. Then, gritting her teeth with determination, she rang the bell for Peg.

The maid took a considerable time in coming. Susan supposed that one of the footmen must have had to track the wayward girl down wherever she had been loitering. As soon as Peg entered the room, however, she began talking about the "Lunnon" gentleman who had come that evening. Brushing her comments aside with impatience, Susan gave her the folded note and asked for her attention. "Peg, you must take zis note to ze stables for me. It is for Tom. I want 'im to bring ze carriage around slightly later in ze morning zan we 'ad agreed upon. But do not dally now," she said as the girl's eyes lit up annoyingly. "I will not 'ave 'im distracted from 'is work."

"Yes, mum," said Peg, for once not resenting an order. "I'll just 'op on down this minute. 'Is 'igh and mighty 'ighness from Lunnon might like to know I've been out for a bit in the stables. It won't do 'im no 'arm to wonder now, will it?" She seemed to be thinking along to herself without regard for Susan, and indeed, Susan's thoughts were too busily occupied to admit of Peg's nonsense. So she ignored the girl and was merely thankful that the one certainty about her was her eagerness to see Tom.

There is no danger he will not get the message, she thought to herself bitterly as Peg skipped out of the room. Now I shall only have to worry about whether he can rid himself of her before midnight.

Susan took a book and tried to keep herself awake reading it until Tom could find his way to her room. She did not worry whether he would be able to enter, for Lady Mewhinny kept the outer door near the stable unlocked until well past midnight. Her servants were not restricted in their movements as they were in some large manors, and Susan had been surprised to see Vigor in unexpected corners of the house.

The one worry that did occupy her mind was that Tom might misinterpret her message. When the idea first occurred to her, she dismissed it as nonsense. Then she recalled Tom's look as he had bade her goodbye in the stables. Would he think she had invited him with some impropriety in mind? The thought was most disturbing and set her heart to beating queerly. It took the exercise of all her good sense to compose her mind. But she told herself firmly that once his lordship had been apprised of the situation—and she would advise him instantly upon his entering—he would understand the need for her action. She hoped she could count on his gallantry not to take too great a notice of her lack of propriety.

But Susan's book did not manage to capture her interest, for her thoughts were in too lively a whirl to settle down to reading. Long before the appointed hour, she had begun to pace the floor, worrying that Tom might not find his way to the correct room. She had not thought to give him proper instructions, and the idea of his being found in the upper corridors without an excuse was enough to drive her to distraction. And the notion that he might be expecting a seduction continued to plague her.

At twenty minutes before the hour, however, there was a light knock at her door, and she ran to open it wide, letting out a gasp at the sight which greeted her eyes.

"Lady Mewhinny!" she cried, seeing her tiny hostess in the doorway. "What are you doing here?" Fortunately, this peculiar greeting did nothing to put off her ladyship, who looked Susan over with similar surprise and concern.

"Why, Susan!" she said, uttering little sounds of disapproval and stepping into the room. "You are not even dressed for bed. Is anything the matter, dear?"

Susan looked down at her own dress as if she were unaware of what she was wearing. "*Non*, noz'ing, Kitty," she said, thinking quickly. "Really noz'ing. I was just putting ze final touches to my packing and I quite forgot ze hour. It is so 'ard to settle down ze night before a journey. Do you not agree?"

Lady Mewhinny nodded wisely in agreement. "Of course, dear. I see how it must be. Your mind is quite taken up with all the little details and is so afraid of forgetting something. But you mustn't worry. If I find you have forgotten anything, I will send it on after you. You must only leave me your address."

"S'ank you," said Susan, wondering what address she might leave and listening at the same time for Lord

Harleston. She raised her voice and spoke more clearly in case he should be already coming down the corridor. "But what are you doing up at zis hour, Kitty? Is anys'ing ze matter?"

"Oh, no, dear," said Lady Mewhinny kindly. "I am never asleep this early in the evening. I thought I might just come along and see if your candle was still lit, for I did not have a proper chance to say goodbye to you before. It has been such a treat for me having you here. You are such a delightful girl."

Susan's heart experienced a sharp pang upon hearing these kind words, but she reminded herself she would not really be going and that Lord Harleston was at this moment making his way to her room.

"Zat was so good of you, Kitty," she said feigning a yawn. "I, too, shall be sorry to leave. I'm so glad you managed to catch me, for I was just about to put out ze light."

Lady Mewhinny smiled and looked about the room. The bed was still buried in its deep, down coverlets. She turned back to Susan with an enquiring look. "But where are your nightclothes, dear?"

Susan flushed, looking about her as if they had suddenly been mislaid, and stammered a reply, "I—I must 'ave packed zem wiz'out s'inking. But no matter. I shall just 'ave to dig zem out again." She hoped that would satisfy her hostess and moved quickly toward the door to show her out, but Lady Mewhinny remained firmly rooted to the floor.

"Oh, no, you mustn't do that, Susan. Why, I am certain to have something you could wear right here in one of these chests." And to Susan's dismay, she began to rummage in one of the huge chests at the foot of the bed, asking her to hold the top while she searched almost to the bottom. At last she emerged, pulling out a flimsy silk confection in white with deep pink roses embroidered upon it. "There," she said with satisfaction. "That ought to suit you to perfection. It had a matching pink dressing gown, as I recall. Sir William got it for me in Paris." She dove back in the chest and recovered the missing item with a cheerful, "Aha!"

Susan looked up at the rococo clock beside the bed and discovered it was almost midnight. In a panic, she nearly snatched the garments from Lady Mewhinny's hands, scarcely taking time to thank her. "Zose will do admirably, Kitty, s'ank you. But I must not keep you from your bed. I promise we shall 'ave time to say our goodbyes in ze morning."

Lady Mewhinny consented to move toward the door, but she noticed Susan's hurry and attributed it to nervousness. Turning on the doorstep she said, "I will bid you good-night, my dear, but I do not think you will be able to sleep without something to soothe your nerves. I will send Simmons up to help you. She has a wonderfully comforting way about her." And before Susan could open her mouth to protest, Lady Mewhinny was halfway down the hall.

Susan, now in anguish, watched her hostess step briskly away. She looked both up and down the corridor, hoping to warn Lord Harleston before he should be seen, but as yet, there was no sign of him. Her stomach churning, she glanced down at the flimsy garments in her hands and buried her face in them with a groan. A delicate aroma of lavender filled her nostrils as the cool silk touched her cheeks. She wanted nothing more than to put them on and abandon herself to luxury, but the fear of Lord Harleston's coming at just the wrong moment—or, worse, of not coming at all—jerked her back to reality.

She kept her vigil until a shuffling sound indicated the approach of Mrs. Simmons. Simmons was Lady Mewhinny's dresser, whom Susan had seen on only one occasion. Aside from Vigor and Lady Mewhinny, she was the oldest person on the estate, and Susan had little confidence in her ability to finish anything in short order.

But surprisingly, within minutes of her coming, Susan found herself seated in front of the mirror, fully robed in the silky dressing gown with a brush being drawn through her hair.

"It's a pleasure to dress you, miss," said Simmons, according her no more status than did Peg. "It's been a long time since I had the pleasure of dressing a pretty lady like yourself. Lady Mewhinny, bless her, is beginning to get on in years." She shook her head a little sadly and then reapplied herself to her work.

"S'ank you, Simmons," said Susan kindly. It was impossible not to be a little seduced by the luxury of having her hair combed for her. Not once had she been tempted to request the service from Peg. "Lady Mewhinny was right. You do 'ave a sooz'ing touch." She cut her off reluctantly with a sigh. "But I must not keep you from your bed. It is quite late and you shouldn't have to stay up on my account." It seemed to her that she had said the same words repeatedly.

"It's no bother, miss," insisted Simmons. "I've already seen to her ladyship's toilet, so I can retire as soon as I've finished here. It's done me good to see these garments put to such good use. I've been keeping them packed in lavender, you see, and they're just as good as new." Then she added with a sigh, "It's too bad your poor late husband could not see you dressed the way you are."

Susan swallowed in renewed panic. The clock beside her bed showed after twelve and Lord Harleston would be coming soon. She must get out of these clothes before he came.

Jumping to her feet, she thanked Mrs. Simmons, trying to sound as relaxed and ready for bed as she could. Fortunately, Lady Mewhinny's servant was easier to get rid of than her mistress, and Susan soon watched her shuffle down the hall.

Quickly Susan shut the door behind her and started to undress again, but before she could do more than remove her wrapper, there came another tap upon the door. She froze. In a moment, the tap came louder.

"Who is it?" she called in a faint voice, struggling to put back on her dressing gown.

"It's Tom!"

Susan cringed at the sound of his voice, which seemed loud enough to wake the whole household. Hurrying to prevent him from calling out again, she unlatched the bolt, opened the door and drew him quickly into the room.

He started to speak in a humorous tone of voice. "Were you, perhaps, expecting someone else...?" Then he stopped, as though he had been struck speechless by the sight of her.

Susan felt herself colour to the roots of her hair. His lordship was standing as if paralyzed. His eyes combed her from head to toe, taking in the luxuriant flow of her long, black hair as well as the obvious curves beneath their flimsy covering. He had not yet noticed the seductive opulence of their surroundings. He had carried his boots to move noiselessly in stockinged feet, but had dropped them after one look at her. They lay disregarded on the floor.

"This is not what it seems, my lord," began Susan hastily, and then chided herself inwardly for putting thoughts into his head which might not already have been there. "I had to see you most urgently, but then Lady Mewhinny came and insisted upon sending her dresser..." She faltered. Lord Harleston's expression did not alter; he seemed not to have heard a word. *You might make this simpler for me,* Susan thought.

All at once, her embarrassment became so intolerable that it flashed into flustered anger. She drew herself up with dignity and stamped her foot, whispering viciously, "Stop staring at me and listen, you great gaping hayseed!" Lord Harleston's eyes flickered as if he suddenly recalled where he was. But to Susan's amazement, he did not blush, but allowed a bovine grin to spread slowly across his face.

"Ur," said his lordship.

Susan's hand flew to her mouth and she started to giggle. Lord Harleston's eyes lit with humour and he reached out as if to take her in his arms, when another tap came softly at the door.

"Susan?" called Lady Mewhinny's voice again from the corridor.

The two inside jumped in sudden horror. "You must hide! Quickly!" squeaked Susan in a whisper, waving her hands wildly away from the door. "I'm coming, Kitty," she called out hastily as Lord Harleston took a quick look round the room.

There was nothing in the elaborate room large enough to conceal him but the great, four-posted bed. Crossing the floor in two strides, he tossed back the covers and hid himself beneath their folds. Susan ran on tiptoe after him to make certain he was thoroughly covered and then walked the way back to the door.

"Yes, Kitty?" she asked nervously as she opened the door to greet her ladyship. Lady Mewhinny had donned an odd-looking cap and carried a candle in her hands.

"I've just come to make sure you were settled, dear. You seemed strangely pale this evening and I wanted to make certain you were comfortable." She held her candle high over her head and took in the rumpled bedclothes. "Oh, I see I've got you out of your bed. I'm so sorry."

Susan opened her mouth to deny it, but remembering the look of the covers stopped herself in time. "It is quite all right, Kitty. It was so kind of you to send your dresser to me. It was such a s'oughtful idea of *yours*." She spoke the last word quite clearly and hoped Lord Harleston heard it. It still mortified her to think he suspected her of trying to seduce him.

Lady Mewhinny smiled at her lovingly. "It was nothing, dearest Susan. I'm so happy to see you looking better. I was not half so lovely in that wrapper as you. Now, you are certain you are all right?" she asked as Susan continued to shift her eyes nervously.

"Perfectly, Kitty," she said firmly. She held her breath as Lady Mewhinny's eyes swept the room. Happily, they seemed to overlook the unusual bulk of the covers, pausing only for a moment as they reached the floor. But in another moment her ladyship looked up as if to go.

"Yes. I can see that you are quite well, my dear. I needn't have worried. Forgive me for bothering you. I shall be off now," she finished as she presented her cheek for a kiss.

Susan obliged her gratefully and closed the door behind her back. Then, as soon as her ladyship's footsteps had disappeared down the hall, she ran back to the bed and called out quietly, "Tom!" At first there was no response and she thought about rifling the bedclothes to search for him, but remembering the curious gleam in his eye, she thought better of it and took a step back from the bed.

"Tom!" she said louder.

Lord Harleston's face appeared slowly from beneath the covers. Unrepentant, he stretched, then yawned slowly and rolled over to face her, his head resting upon his hand.

Susan watched him with fascination, then started suddenly and perched herself primly upon a chair. "As you perhaps heard, Tom—Lord Harleston, that is—" Susan blushed with annoyance "—Lady Mewhinny's dresser came to my room just as I was expecting you and insisted upon putting me into this costume. It is not at all what it appears."

His lordship looked at her sadly and sighed. "It's not?"

"Of course not," said Susan, sitting as straight in her chair as she could. The room was chilly and a draft was blowing across her bare feet.

Lord Harleston sighed again. He looked absurdly disappointed. "I thought not," he said.

If possible, Susan was even more mortified by his response. "You didn't . . . ?" she ventured.

Tom opened his eyes with a great show of innocence, "The thought never crossed my mind," he said unconvincingly.

Susan could no longer meet his eyes. "Lord Harleston," she said in a pleading tone, "You could not possibly have thought that I—"

His voice cut across hers kindly, "What is it you needed to speak to me about so urgently, Miss Johnstone?"

She looked up and saw his teasing gaze upon her. Suddenly all was right; she should have known he was only roasting her.

"Oh, Lord Harleston," she said, recalling her worries of earlier in the evening. It seemed hours ago that she had thought of sending for him. "It is Lady Mewhinny's nephew, Mr. Petworthy! He is planning something horrid, I know! I overheard him talking to his guest, Mr. Sodporth, and they were speaking of Lady Mewhinny in the most disrespectful fashion. He wants her money and I am so afraid he plans to kill her!" Susan went on to describe the dinner table conversation and to give Lord Harleston an accurate account of what she had overheard.

He listened to her with his brows drawn together in a frown of concentration. When she had finished, he asked, "Have you told Lady Mewhinny about this?"

Susan shook her head miserably. "I couldn't. You see, I have no proof other than my own word. And *that*," she added wryly, "cannot be worth much. Oh, I hate practising this deception upon her!"

Lord Harleston sat upright upon the bed and leaned over to take her hands in his. "You must not blame yourself for that. It cannot be helped. But you are right that we must not do anything to bring questions down upon ourselves that cannot be answered satisfactorily. It will not help Lady Mewhinny in the long run. Did you say she was fond of this scoundrel?''

Susan frowned slightly. ''I cannot say for certain. She seems totally unconcerned. And she does not seem to mind having him or his guest here, in spite of the fact that he is quite hostile to her monkeys.''

Lord Harleston raised his brows expressively. ''Lord, yes. I'd forgotten the monkeys. It is just possible,'' he suggested gently, ''that Lady Mewhinny is getting too old to cope with her affairs.''

Susan shifted uncomfortably. ''I ought to agree, I suppose,'' she admitted, ''but it does not seem that way at all. She is always so brisk and businesslike. Oh, she may be rather peculiar at times, but I get the impression it is because her mind is on so many things at once.''

Lord Harleston smiled tolerantly to himself and dropped the line of conversation. ''So what is it you wish me to do?'' he asked.

All at once Susan became aware that her hands still rested in his. She stole a quick look at his face. In it she could read his readiness to do her bidding. She realized she had seldom seen him when he was not in a joking humour, but his willingness always to come to her aid touched her deeply. Gently, she removed her hands from his clasp.

''Lord Harleston,'' she began, ''I had to speak to you right away to tell you that I must not leave tomorrow. I cannot leave Lady Mewhinny alone to deal with Mr. Petworthy. He said quite clearly that he would be glad to witness my departure, that my presence was a hindrance to his plans."

"What do you mean to do?"

Susan's thoughts were a mass of confusion. "I do not know," she admitted. "But surely something will occur to me when I know what his intentions are."

"Well, then," said his lordship cheerfully, reclining once more on the bed. "We shall just have to skulk about and spy on the fellow until we know what he is up to."

Susan's eyes opened wide with astonishment. Ignoring his impudent posture, she rose to her feet and took a step nearer. "But you cannot mean to stay on, too! You cannot possibly wish to prolong this masquerade!"

"Why not?" asked his lordship, regarding her with a half smile.

"Because . . ." Susan groped for words. "You cannot! Just think how uncomfortable you've been!"

Lord Harleston looked down his long body as it lay atop the billowing covers. His eyes took in the seductive paintings around him, the elaborate ceiling, the curved furniture. "But look how comfortable I am now," he said. "It seems to me," he added, looking slowly up at Susan as she stood beside him, "that it is *you* who are most uncomfortable."

An absurd response drifted into Susan's mind before she could take in his meaning. Her feet *were* getting chilled. "Nonsense!" she replied hastily, turning her back to him before the temptation could be too great. Her voice sounded sulky.

Lord Harleston rose immediately to his feet. "Please forgive me, Miss Johnstone," he said in all seriousness. "I should return your bed to you. It was unforgiveable of me to keep it while you stood there shivering."

Susan *was* shivering, she suddenly realized. But she doubted it was from the cold, for his lordship's approach had only made it worse. Thanking him, she reached round him for one of the covers and draped it over her shoulders. He helped her to arrange it until it hung like a great cape about her feet.

"Thank you," she said again timidly and then continued in a pleading tone, "But Lord Harleston, you must not stay on to help Lady Mewhinny! I am aware my own impulsiveness has a tendency to get me into trouble, but I do not wish to embroil you further in my scrapes. I will not have it!"

"Of course you won't," he said, wrapping the coverlet more closely about her and speaking as though he were comforting a child. "But you forget, I gave my oath to your father. And," he added, as she seemed about to protest, "I should be a pretty poor fellow if I were unwilling to come to the assistance of a frail old lady, now. Would I not?"

Susan smiled wistfully up at him. She could not know how dangerously she upset his restraint by doing so.

"But, my lord . . ." He silenced her with an uplifted hand. She wanted to object, but the words caught in her throat. Tears of gratitude mingled with guilt and frustration were choking her, and she was afraid to release them. She feared what might happen if he comforted her in their present situation.

Lord Harleston quickly made as if to go, promising to devise their excuse by morning. "There is one more thing," he said, turning as he reached the door. "We shall have to meet rather frequently to report our findings to each other, I suppose?"

"I suppose so," agreed Susan.

"Just so," he said. His manner appeared business-like. "Then we must think of a place to meet." His brow wrinkled as if he were pondering the matter.

Susan watched him shyly. "I could come more often into the stables," she offered.

He threw her a quick, impish smile. "I rather prefer this location," he said, "but I see it might not be the most practical spot."

She bent her head in confusion, a rosy warmth invading her. But as her glance swept the floor, she stopped at the sight of his boots and her mood turned instantly to one of alarm.

"Your boots!" she cried. "Oh, Tom, you left your boots! Do you think Lady Mewhinny could have seen them?"

Lord Harleston looked quickly down, momentarily distracted from her use of his first name. "Damn," he said mildly. "That was careless of me. But she could not have seen them or she would have said something, surely?'' He looked to her for agreement.

Susan sighed with relief. "Of course. How silly of me. She must have said something if she had noticed. I daresay her eyesight is not what it was for I am certain she looked this way." Then she added with a dimple, "But they are so big and loutish, it is a miracle she did not see them."

Lord Harleston tried to appear offended, but the look he gave her only served to make her dimple more. "Very well, my lady," he said. "I shall not stay here to be insulted any further, but shall betake myself to my crude pallet where I shall endeavour to sleep in as unloutish a fashion as possible. I shall await your pleasure in the morning."

Susan, despite the teasing nature of his words, was instantly contrite. The thought of his sleeping on a wooden pallet was enough to make her think foolishly of offering him her bed. But fortunately, Lord Harleston closed the door before she could make this imprudent offer. A second later its impropriety struck her.

"Heavens!" she said aloud, one hand flying to her forehead. "What on earth was I about to say?"

A glance down at her clothing reminded her of the strangeness of her situation, and she fled back to her bed and hid herself under the covers. She ought, she told herself, to feel quite worried about Lady Mewhinny and Mr. Petworthy. And she ought to be ashamed that she had not persuaded Lord Harleston to leave. But somehow she only felt a delicious thrill as she wriggled down deeper in the bed. A sudden prickle made her sit up and search about with her hand for its source. It was a piece of straw.

Smiling tenderly, she lay back down and drew the straw beneath her nostrils. It had a faint scent, so she could almost imagine she was in the stables with Tom. As long as she lived, she knew, that smell would remind her of Lord Harleston. Over her head, amidst swirls of gilt and flowers, nymphs and satyrs cavorted on the ceiling. But tonight they did not embarrass her. She was beginning to understand them, she thought rather naughtily.

Lord Harleston's manner had been almost perfect. He had kept his distance, as a gentleman under those circumstances should, but he had made it quite clear he would not have minded in the least if the invitation to her chamber had been for more.

CHAPTER NINE

THE NEXT MORNING, Tom duly made his announcement that the carriage was in need of repair and would take a number of days to be fixed. Lady Mewhinny expressed her delight at being allowed to keep Susan a few more days, and Mr. Petworthy was obliged to swallow his irritation.

"We shall count ourselves fortunate to be amongst such pleasant company, shall we not, Sodporth?" he said, smiling at Susan through clenched teeth.

They were at the breakfast table, where, much to Susan's discomfort, the gentlemen had appeared as early as she and Lady Mewhinny were wont to do. Mr. Sodporth beamed upon her, but did not reply owing to the fullness of his mouth. His host was not so speechless, however.

"It would seem your household will be obliged to suffer a certain degree of alarm on your behalf," he said. "I cannot believe they are used to such extraordinary delays in your arrival." The look he directed at her was full of suspicion.

Alarmed to see that her motives for staying were already open to doubt, Susan was forced to reply with a false degree of composure, "Tom will 'ave sent word to my 'ousekeeper zat we are unavoidably detained, but it does not really matter. Zere is no one to whom my movements can have ze least importance.''

"Indeed!" said Mr. Petworthy, still smiling with his lips only. He looked as if he might have asked her more uncomfortable questions, but Lady Mewhinny cut into this conversation with bright cheeriness.

"I am so happy you are staying, my dear Susan, for now you will be able to accompany me to the opening of Heffel Fair tomorrow."

Mr. Petworthy watched Susan closely as he observed, "Surely not, Aunt. Why, have you forgotten our guest is in mourning? She will not wish to appear so unaffected by her loss."

Susan did not like the look he gave her. But in spite of being alarmed at the prospect of being left behind at the house without Lady Mewhinny's protective presence, she could not deny his statement.

"Oh, dear. What a pity, to be sure!" said Lady Mewhinny. "But perhaps your mourning is of long standing, my dear. I do not recall your having mentioned the exact time of your bereavement."

Susan thought rapidly. "It was a mere year ago last monz', my lady."

Lady Mewhinny brightened considerably. "There you see! I am so glad to hear it. It is high time you put off your mourning then, dear. No one will think the worse of you at your age. You will undoubtedly marry again. And, of course, here no one will be the wiser.

Let us go up to your room right away and see what you have that is suitable.''

Susan looked doubtfully around the table as if uncertain whether she ought to be so hasty, but Mr. Petworthy only bowed in chilly acquiescence. So, suppressing her eagerness, she rose from the table and went to join her ladyship.

Lady Mewhinny appeared to find nothing odd about Susan's carrying with her certain dresses which were not black. She had one gown, the one she had taken to London to visit her father in prison, which the elderly lady declared to be the very thing. It had been Susan's last extravagance at a time when Captain Johnstone had still been hopeful of restoring his fortune. He had sent her a portion of his winnings at the table with instructions to purchase herself a new gown. She remembered the wording of his letter still:

My dear Susan,
I shall not be able to come to you in May as we had planned in our last exchange of letters. I find matters here in Town demand my attendance. I am hopeful, however, that I shall soon be in a position to reestablish our household in a more tolerable degree of elegance. Rest assured you will not be obliged to impose on Miss Iron's hospitality much longer.

The following paragraph had sounded even more hopeful:

By way of assuaging whatever disappointment
you may feel at my not being able to come into
Hertfordshire, I am sending you a small portion
by way of a gift. To please me you must use it to
increase your wardrobe, for you will soon be in
need of more garments suitable to our coming
change in circumstances. You may tell Miss Irons
that I feel certain of being in a position to repay
her for her hospitality within a number of days.

Your affectionate father,
James Johnstone

Looking at the dress now, Susan remembered how
sadly she had received the news of his not coming, but
Miss Irons had insisted upon her buying a new gown
with the money. And they had both been sufficiently
encouraged by Captain Johnstone's letter to believe
that she would soon have a use for her new purchase.
But no further word was heard from the Captain for
more than six months, and when he finally wrote he
made no mention of his previous allusions to im-
proved circumstances. Miss Irons was never repaid for
her expenditures, and Susan had never regarded her
father's subsequent promises as having any basis other
than in his own optimism.

The dress, although a few years out of date, was a
lovely white muslin with a pale blue, three-quarter-
length tunic laid over in silk. Pale pink embroidery in
a classical design adorned the square neckline of the

tightly fitted tunic. The sleeves were puffed, and blue fringe completed the hem.

The next day, wearing her dress and a cape borrowed from Lady Mewhinny and feeling absurdly frivolous, Susan stepped up into the ancient carriage which was to take her and her ladyship to the fair. Mr. Petworthy had decided to accompany them, but perhaps feeling their equipage to be something beneath his dignity, suggested following them in his own. Vigor was seated atop the box, but even though Susan looked about her, she could see no sign of Tom.

Sighing, she took her place beside Lady Mewhinny and tried not to be sorry that Lord Harleston had not seen her in her finery.

"Do you always attend ze opening of ze fair, Kitty?" she asked.

To her surprise, Lady Mewhinny smiled rather self-consciously and shook her head. "Not always, my dear," she said. "In fact, this is rather a special occasion, which makes me doubly glad you are to accompany me. You see, it is a local tradition that the first cuckoo of spring shall be released at Heffel Fair. The people are quite superstitious about it and insist that it must be done by an old woman. Up until now, the innkeeper's mother was the eldest woman in the village, but she died just last autumn. So after much discussion, the mayor of Heathfield approached me to perform the service at this year's fair."

Susan smiled inwardly at the idea of the mayor's approaching her on a matter of such delicacy and im-

portance. "I am certain zey will all be honoured at
your condescending to do it, Kitty. Is 'effel Fair a large
one, zen? I do not s'ink I 'ave ever 'eard it mentioned." Susan forgot that as a Frenchwoman she
could hardly have been expected to know it.

The notion did not trouble Lady Mewhinny, however, for she shook her head sadly and replied. "No,
it is not very large, I'm afraid, although it once was
many years ago. How dearly I remember the fairs in
those days, when the Weald was the site of all the
forges in England. You would not believe it now, Susan, but the sound of the great hammers could be
heard in every village, and the hammer ponds were
great scenes of activity. That was before they used
coal. There is only one forge left now, not near here,
and nothing left of the forest. It was all burned to feed
the forges. And I'm afraid Heffel Fair will not be with
us much longer. The gentry have other ways of enter-
taining themselves in these days and do not look so
kindly upon the amusements of the lower classes."

She smiled rather wistfully, and Susan was sad-
dened to think that the world of Lady Mewhinny's
girlhood had faded so far into the past.

They were greeted at the fair by an assortment of
village dignitaries, and Susan observed with interest
that Mr. Petworthy did not stay with them. Instead, he
took himself off with his friend, the doctor, and
seemed to give them no further thought.

Lady Mewhinny, supported on the arm of Vigor,
was led up to a sort of stage in the middle of the fes-

tivities. Susan stayed nearby long enough to watch her ladyship release the caged bird and then, as the proclamation was read officially declaring the opening of the fair, decided to take a look round.

In spite of its reduced size since the time of its heyday, Heffel Fair still offered many sights to amaze. There was no longer a special day for the gentry, or specific days for trade. Instead, Susan saw a mixture of persons from the local Jacks and Mollys to the tradesmen and farmers there on the important business of the fair. In the distance, she could see the sheep pens and a few workhorses for sale; beside her were all the booths and tents set up for amusement.

A bold sign advertised the horrifying sight of a male child born with a bear growing on his back, alive. Music, a rather discordant blend from trumpets, fiddles and beaten calfskins, emerged from the Musick Booth where, it was promised, would later be given a dramatization of the French Revolution. Puppets would be guillotined. The Market House was occupied by the butchers' shops and other culinary shops, while around it were booths for prizefighting, juggling and wild beasts offered for sale.

"Here is your nice gingerbread, your spice gingerbread," called a voice behind her. As she turned the vendor held out a star-shaped packet of the hot, spicy bread, wrapped in Dutch gold. "It will melt in your mouth like a red-hot brickbat and rumble in your inside like Punch in his wheelbarrow. Want some, miss?"

Susan's mouth watered at the smells coming from his basket of different-shaped delicacies. She would have given almost anything at that moment to purchase the sweet molasses-filled treat, but prudence asserted itself. She must not use what little remained of her father's fifty pounds on luxuries, however small. She sighed and shook her head regretfully and the vendor moved on.

She was passing between two tents on her way to look at the horses, when a hand suddenly reached out and drew her back behind them. She would have cried out, had she not immediately seen who her assailant was.

"Lord Harleston!" she exclaimed, smiling happily upon seeing him. "What are you doing here?"

The sun was shining down upon his fair hair and seemed reflected in his eyes as he responded to her greeting, "Vigor told me you would be coming to the fair with Lady Mewhinny this morning and I hoped I might have a chance to see you. It seemed as good a place as any to chance a meeting."

Susan flushed with pleasure. "Yes, it is." She was conscious of his eyes upon her. They took in her festive dress with one glance and she could not be doubtful of his admiration. She hastily explained, "Lady Mewhinny encouraged me to put off my mourning for the fair. She thinks Mr. Faringdon is more than a year deceased, you see." She could not help a flirtatious note from creeping into her speech.

"Is he, now?" said Tom. "Well, I cannot pretend to be sorry for it."

His words made her heart beat rapidly. It is the fair, she thought. It was infecting them both.

She changed the subject hastily. "Have you seen Mr. Petworthy? He is here this morning and I must be careful. He is acting as if his suspicions are aroused. Have you found anything about him?"

"Not yet," said his lordship unconcernedly. "But it is early yet. Perhaps I will be able to learn something from his manservant, a particularly nasty fellow, but not overly fond of his master, I gather. In the meantime, however, I have been busy."

His look prompted her to enquire as to his meaning, and he answered with a curiously sheepish pride. "If you must know," he said jokingly, "I, like the cleverest of the three pigs, got up early this morning and preceded the wolf to the fair. Since you were nowhere in evidence, I decided to try my hand at a boxing match. And I won a prize."

And here he produced from the pocket of his breeches a set of hair ribbons in royal blue. Susan laughed at the proud expression on his face. "I did not know they awarded hair ribbons for such valour," she asserted pertly.

For once, Tom seemed to abandon his impudence. "They don't...or not precisely. I was given my choice of prizes: a pint or a choice of trinkets. I could not think any of the objects I saw would serve you in the least except perhaps these ribbons. They could go with that lovely gown you're wearing, I suppose." He held them out to her and Susan took them in silence.

She stared at the silken strands for a moment before, unwilling to meet his eye, she ventured a shy, "Thank you." But she was thinking at the same time that she had never received a more precious gift. "I shall have to put them in my reticule for now," she apologized, "for I do not have a glass to see myself with. But I shall look forward to wearing them on the next occasion of my wearing this dress." The thought occurred to her that the next time she wore it, she would no longer be in his company.

Lord Harleston cleared his throat and smiled at some private thought of his own. His spirits seemed quite high, as if his adventures of the morning had been unusually promising. Music came from the Musick Booth again with a voice announcing the performance of "a young woman who dances with fourteen glasses on the backs and palms of her hands while turning as fast as a windmill." The music resembled that of a country dance.

"If I really were Tom, the groom," said Susan's companion, "and you were a lady's maid, we might have come here together unbeknownst to our mistress to dance in the music tent." Susan lifted her chin and gazed at him invitingly. His eyes gleamed as he bowed and held out one hand. She took it, for once not worrying if they might be seen. In truth, the shelter of the tents was rather like a private ballroom where they might indulge their sudden whim in perfect seclusion.

Tom led her to the end of their imaginary set and Susan immediately forgot the rudeness of their surroundings. To be dancing this way with Lord Harleston could not have been more magical if they had been at the ballroom at Almack's, or if they had really been two truants from service. The music stopped, but resumed quickly with a waltz. Tom did not hesitate, but swooped her up with his right arm and guided her into the dance.

But Susan did not know how to waltz, and the abrupt change in pattern quickly woke her to their setting. She did not have his experience of the fashionable world, and a few brief episodes at country assemblies when she was younger had not prepared her for the breathtaking experience of being guided by a man's arm. Almost too shaken then to speak, she gently but firmly disengaged herself from his embrace and, staring at him wide-eyed, said, "Thank you very much, my lord. But I had best be getting back to Lady Mewhinny. She will be wondering what has become of me."

He returned her stare, but it seemed to her his eyes were full of regret. "Very well," he said. "It is time for my lady's maid to resume her identity as Mrs. Faringdon. Next time we are forced into such a masquerade, however, I trust I will have the sense to place us in more equal roles. The ups and downs of this business are rather unsettling."

Susan flushed and pretended to ignore the true meaning of his words. "There will be no more masquerades, my lord,'' she insisted. ''Do you not realize that I could hang for what I did? And what would become of your reputation if you were known to have helped me? You might be prosecuted yourself!''

He took her hand and gazed at her earnestly. ''Nothing of the sort is going to happen. I have been thinking of what to do for some time, and I am almost certain a pardon can be obtained for you. It may take time, but I shall start working on it as soon as I get back to London.''

Susan's heart leapt with hope and then sank again. ''Lord Harleston, you must not say such things. For one moment—but I know it will be impossible.''

''But the Regent . . .''

''No!'' insisted Susan. ''You must not. Please! You must not speak of me to anyone. Only think of the consequences if you are mistaken. I'm afraid your imagination has got the better of you, but you must be careful. I have too great a—'' her voice faltered ''—too great a regard for you to allow you to disgrace yourself because of me.'' Her gaze fell as she noticed the sudden spark of hope in his eyes.

She spoke hurriedly, ''I must get back to Lady Mewhinny.'' Susan turned around and started to step back between the tents, Lord Harleston following behind her. But before she emerged, she spied Mr. Petworthy and stopped hastily, almost falling back into his lordship's arms.

"It is Lady Mewhinny's nephew," she explained in a whisper. "I must not let him see me coming out from here."

They watched him silently. Mr. Petworthy was making his way toward the sheep pens, glancing occasionally over his shoulder as if to make certain there was no one following him. His manner was decidedly suspicious. His friend, Mr. Sodporth, was nowhere in evidence.

"I think I should follow him," said Lord Harleston in a low voice. "Who knows, but what he might be meeting someone here and I could pick up a bit of knowledge."

Susan responded eagerly, "Then I will come, too."

Tom smiled down at her. "I do not think that would be best," he suggested. "He is not very likely to notice me, a groom, but you are already under suspicion. I will let you know as soon as possible if I find out anything."

But Susan would not let him leave her out of the adventure. "I must come with you," she said earnestly. "I promise to conceal myself, but I must learn what he has in mind to do to poor Kitty."

"All right," he agreed after a pause, "but we will have to find shelter if we want to get close enough to hear."

They waited for Mr. Petworthy to pass out of sight before emerging from their place between the tents, but as soon as they had walked a few yards, they caught up with him. He had stopped before the sheep pens and was looking around, consulting his watch occasionally as if expecting someone.

"I must get to the other side of those pens," said Lord Harleston, drawing Susan back with a hand on her elbow. "Will you go back to Lady Mewhinny?"

Susan shook her head. "No. I am coming with you."

He glanced down at her dress regretfully. "I am afraid you may spoil your gown," he warned.

But Susan was not to be deterred. "Nonsense. I shall be quite careful. And I shall not persist if my being along prevents you from getting close enough to hear him."

He nodded. "Good girl. Let's see if we can get round here." And leading her back along the way they had come, he took a narrow path which seemed to skirt the animal pens. Before long they were passing along the outside of the village where it opened into meadow. Lord Harleston followed closely along the fences which confined the animals until they caught sight of Mr. Petworthy's soberly clad figure. Someone whom neither of them knew, had joined him, and the two men were in close conversation.

Lord Harleston squatted behind a fence post and pulled Susan down with him. "I see nothing for it but for me to enter the pen. This one appears to be empty and it should be close enough at the front for me to hear them if I can get quite into the corner. You must stay here."

"If it is empty, I see no reason why I might not come, too," said Susan reasonably, or so she thought. Her companion started to protest, but she indicated with an impatient wave of her hand that they had no time to argue the point.

Lord Harleston made no further objection other than to look at her as if to say he hoped she would not regret it. Then, bent over double, he led the way through the gate and along the fence separating their pen from the one in front of which Mr. Petworthy was standing. Susan found it was more difficult to walk doubled over than she had imagined, although she was happy she had not bothered to wear stays.

Fortunately, there had been no rain for the past few days, so the floor of the pen was relatively dry. Susan was obliged, however, to hold up her skirts in an awkward manner to avoid brushing them against the filthy straw which covered it. That her slippers would be ruined by the ordeal, she was well aware.

They had just got within a few paces of the corner of the pen, when Mr. Petworthy and his confederate concluded their business together and started off on their separate ways. Lord Harleston stopped his near crawl with a sigh and, still stooping, turned round to face her. It was at that moment that one of the farmers chose to empty a pail into the pen.

He was cleaning out a trough in the next pen of the water left by the sheep. It was murky and slimy with the filth from the animals and filled with pieces of straw from their muzzles. With the help of a large wooden bucket, he had scooped out the remaining water prior to refilling the trough, and it was this that he tossed into the pen.

The majority of the water struck Tom in the head and back, while Susan's lap received the rest of it. Only a quick hand to the mouth sufficed to stifle her scream.

"Ohhh!" she exclaimed, revolted by the muck, but aware at the same time she must be careful to keep her voice down. "Ohhh, Tom!"

But his lordship, after one furious second, decided to laugh. He chuckled, and his amusement was so strong that it threatened to topple him. Instead he rose to his feet, drawing Susan up with him.

"We had best make our way out of this pen or we shall risk being doused again," he said. They hurried out the way they had come, Susan in a constant fright of being seen in such disgrace.

When they were safely out and away from the threat of viewers, Susan let loose with an anguished wail. "Look at my dress! Oh, Lord Harleston. What shall I do?" She turned to him in distress, but his look of amusement was enough to make her laugh in spite of herself.

"Odious man!" she concluded. "I suppose you will next be saying this was all my doing and that this punishment is well deserved."

"I shall do no such thing," he told her. "It would be most ungentlemanly. But at the same time, you cannot expect me not to be amused. Between us, we present quite a spectacle."

Susan could not deny it. Tom's hair was plastered to his head and the back of his shirt and breeches was soaked with muck. The front of her dress was in a similar state, and was clinging indecently to her body. She hoped the unpleasant nature of the water was keeping him from noticing the latter fact.

"Perfectly odious!" retorted Susan. "But what shall I do? I cannot think Lady Mewhinny so completely nearsighted that she will not perceive my state of disarray! And I must be getting back to the carriage! I have been missing far too long."

He nodded in agreement. But looking round, he spied what appeared to be a brook in the near distance. Pointing it out to her he said, "Let's see if we cannot repair some of the damage." Then, giving her his arm, he made his way over to the water's edge.

"But I have no cloth with which to dab at my clothes," Susan protested. At first Tom seemed not to have heard her, but the next thing she knew he had removed his smock and dipped it in the clear water. It took a moment before the dirty water was rinsed from his own garment, but as soon as it began to take on a whiter colour, he wrung it with his hands and presented it to her.

"You will still be quite wet," he said, "but at least the filth can be got out." He smiled up at her in a reassuring way which somehow set her heart to fluttering.

She took the wet shirt in her hand and scrubbed the front of her gown vigorously. It would not come as clean as his shirt had from being submerged, but the worst of the mess did come off. She returned it to him, glancing shyly down at his exposed figure, but observing, "Your hair is quite full of muck, I'm afraid. You really do look the part of the groom much more than I ever thought you would."

His eyes laughed up at her. "*Touché.* I suppose I deserved that for laughing at a lady in distress. But I will still refrain from telling you I told you so."

Susan laughed at his implication. Then, looking back toward the fair, she remarked anxiously, "I must be going. Perhaps if I go straight to the carriage, I can say that I had been waiting for her to arrive. I will say I found myself on the wrong side of the ducking pond at just the wrong moment, and made my way immediately back to the carriage to avoid the embarrassment of being seen in this state."

"Sounds an excellent explanation to me," said Lord Harleston. "And I shall walk back in this direction." He waved toward the opposite side of the brook.

They parted and Susan made her way back to the fair, unaware that his lordship's eyes followed her as far as they could with an expression of total satisfaction.

Luckily, she was the first one to reach the carriage. Within minutes, however, Lady Mewhinny and Vigor returned, having searched for her all over the fair without success. Her ladyship was effusive with her exclamations of distress over finding Susan in such a state, and greatly feared the accident had spoiled her enjoyment of the fête.

But Susan assured her it had not, and her countenance was so full of pleasure at the recollection of dancing with Lord Harleston behind the tents, that Lady Mewhinny could have no doubt on the matter. They rode home in happy silence. Once, Susan caught a glimpse out the window of Tom walking home across the fields, but she trusted her two elderly companions did not notice the similar wetness of his attire.

CHAPTER TEN

THAT EVENING AT DINNER, Mr. Petworthy approached his aunt again about allowing him to manage her affairs. Lady Mewhinny thanked him with as much good cheer as ever but firmly declined. Susan could not like the hint of desperation in Mr. Petworthy's eyes as he heard her final decision, nor did she trust the curt nod which he subsequently gave to his friend. Clearing his throat, Mr. Sodporth began immediately to pose probing questions to her ladyship concerning the care of her monkeys, and since he had shown no other interest in them before, Susan's suspicions were instantly aroused.

"You say you assist the servants in the care of these creatures, Lady Mewhinny?" said the doctor. "Is that not rather strenuous exercise for a lady of your years?"

"You may well wonder, my dear sir," said Lady Mewhinny with a wry glance at him. "But I can assure you it is nothing but a pleasure to me."

Mr. Sodporth shook his head with a suggestion of concern. Then, looking up at Susan with a curiously intent expression, he continued to address her ladyship. "I can only wonder at the motivation for engag-

ing in such a curious pursuit.'' Susan was shocked to
find that the doctor's amiable demeanour had van-
ished, and in its place was a rather calculating look.
Fearfully, she wondered what it could mean.

But her attention was claimed by Mr. Petworthy,
who remarked quietly at her elbow, ''I have often
wondered much the same thing.'' His remark was ac-
companied by a significant look which she was at a
loss to interpret. It seemed as if both gentlemen were
soliciting her agreement on the subject. She wanted to
disavow all similarity of opinion with theirs, but found
she was too distressed to utter a single sound. Or, she
had to admit to herself, to come up with any reasonable comment in support of Lady Mewhinny's actions.

It was with considerable anxiety that Susan made
her way carefully to the stables that afternoon. She felt
she must consult Tom immediately about the sudden
change.

He listened to her with a suitable air of gravity. ''It
certainly seems,'' he agreed, ''as if they were about to
set upon their work, but I cannot conceive of what
would make them concern themselves with your
opinions. And I do not like it! I should not have allowed you to stay up at the house with two such
scoundrels!'' He frowned as if annoyed with himself.

Susan was touched by his concern for her, but dismissed it with assurances. ''It is of no consequence. I
do not think their evil intentions extend to me. It
seems more that they wish to convince me of the cor-
rectness of their own opinions, but as yet, I cannot

imagine what they have in mind. Mr. Sodporth's questions centred mostly on Lady Mewhinny's activities with regard to her monkeys. Do you suppose they intend trying to take them from her?''

Lord Harleston shook his head. ''I do not think so. It does not seem to make any sense. And I have not been successful in extracting any news from his valet. The infernal fellow never seems to be about when I find an excuse to carry me up to the house.''

Susan nodded and thought of Peg, whom she had not seen in the past two days.

''But you must not stay there a moment longer,'' Tom continued. ''We can leave tomorrow and I will send a magistrate to look into the business.''

Susan started to protest but was silenced by Tom's upheld hand. A voice came from near the door to the stables, and it was only by hurried activity that she and he were able to hide themselves before someone entered.

The voice belonged to Mr. Petworthy, who was in company with Mr. Sodporth. From beneath the pile of straw under which Tom had hidden them, Susan could hear the gentlemen's voices clearly.

''Yes, that was my uncle all right, damned spouter! Come to demand his money. I had to tell him some of our plan before he'd consent to give me more time.'' Susan, at first, thought Mr. Petworthy was in possession of another uncle about whom she had not heard, and wondered why he had not called at the manor. But Mr. Petworthy's subsequent remarks cleared up the matter for her.

"Don't ever do business with the moneylenders, Sodporth! They'll bleed you dry, the dirty scoundrels! As if a gentleman hasn't better things to do than worry about paying his bills." The two men stopped in front of the stall where Susan and Lord Harleston were hiding. Unconsciously, Susan moved nearer to him for protection. His arm stole around her and she had to remind herself it was to give her support. Nevertheless, her heart beat so loudly as a result that she was certain the other men must have heard it.

"So what shall we do now?" asked Mr. Sodporth.

"We must proceed with our plan," said his accomplice. "Are you certain of securing the assistance of your friend?"

"Oh, without a doubt," replied Sodporth. "Mr. Smidley often acts without a shade of evidence. You have only to come through with your part of the bargain when the business is concluded. I took the liberty of promising him something in the vicinity of fifty pounds—on your behalf, of course."

Mr. Petworthy growled that he wished his friend would be less generous with money that was not his own, but he was interrupted by Mr. Sodporth.

"You realize, of course, my dear Petworthy, that the signatures of *two* justices of the peace will be required to commit her. The law is more strictly enforced since the committee of enquiry was appointed in recent years. Things are not so easy as they used to be," he finished regretfully.

Susan felt her skin crawl with horror. So that was what all their significant glances had been about! They wanted to send Lady Mewhinny to Bedlam! Or something equally evil, at least. Susan could not think of poor Lady Mewhinny in such a situation without tears springing immediately to her eyes. Only Tom's arm tightening about her kept her from crying out against their infamy.

But Mr. Petworthy was speaking. "Then we must find another signature, and in a hurry! Only my repeated assurances that I would soon be trustee of my aunt's estate sufficed to convince that old beggar to call off the bailiffs. Surely if there is one signature already, the other justice will not feel obliged to delve into the matter very deeply?"

"Probably not," Sodporth agreed. "But I shall endeavour over the next few days to make a note of her ladyship's odd behaviour. It will undoubtedly show signs of monomania. Her sleeplessness is a definite sign."

Mr. Petworthy expressed feelings of satisfaction with his friend's professional opinions and urged him to be quick about the business. Then the two men broke off their meeting and strolled out of the stables.

As soon as they had gone, Susan lifted herself out of the straw and turned to place her hands on Tom's chest. He held them there and listened as she poured forth her anxiety.

"Oh, Tom!" she cried, unaware of the sudden lurch within him. "My poor, dear Lady Mewhinny! We must not let them do this to her! Why, they will have everyone thinking her mad!"

He nodded somewhat distractedly and, releasing one hand began gently to pluck the straw from her hair.

"What shall we do?" she continued, calming unconsciously at the touch of his hand.

Tom looked at her with an expression that was peculiarly apologetic. "I promise you, Susan, word of a gentleman, that I shall not let these rogues hurt Lady Mewhinny," he said, smiling at her trusting look of relief. "But I find myself unable to do anything about it until I have tended to first things first." And with that, he encircled her waist again with a strong arm and swept her into an embrace.

Susan had been so instantly reassured by his promise that she could hardly be ashamed of her reaction. But Tom had said all would be right, so she put both her hands round his neck and indulged in the most exquisite pleasure she had ever known. For a moment, all else was forgotten, and the quickening of her heart, which she had attributed to fear for her ladyship, continued in such a way that she was no longer in doubt as to its cause. And they kept on, bestowing kisses with such tenderness that Susan finally had to break away before she could stand no more.

Lord Harleston held her hands in his while they gazed into each other's eyes. The joy in her own was clearly reflected in his, and she was deliciously disturbed by the rapidity of his breathing. But they had no time to say a word before another voice from the stable door startled them into action.

"My dear Susan!" uttered Lady Mewhinny in shocked tones as Susan hastily snatched her hands away. "What has happened?"

Susan regarded her ladyship in panic as she vainly searched for words to hide her confusion.

"Mrs. Faringdon," began Tom, and then cleared his voice of its hoarseness. "Mrs. Faringdon slipped in the hay as she was coming to give me instructions, and I have just helped her to rise." Susan scarcely expected Lady Mewhinny to accept such a bouncer, but the kindly old lady did not take issue.

"Why, you poor, poor child," she said. "It seems your stay with me has been fraught with such miserable occurrences. And look at your gown!" she exclaimed. "I fear it is ruined."

Susan looked down hurriedly and saw that indeed another of her gowns had been soiled. "I am afraid Tom 'as not cleaned out ze stable properly, Lady Mewhinny," she said, hiding a smile. "I shall 'ave to speak to 'im at once." She allowed herself a glance in his direction, but had to look away quickly to avoid laughing at his false contrition.

"You certainly must!" agreed Lady Mewhinny warmly, "but first you must come with me and see about laundering that dress. I was coming to look for Vigor, but I see he isn't here. Never mind that for now. Come along, dear."

Susan was swept away from the stables without a chance to speak to Lord Harleston about the change which had just come over them. At the door she did venture a glance over her shoulder and found that

Tom was watching her depart with such a look as made her tremble with joy.

But Susan could not long indulge her newfound happiness. Although she did not doubt the strength of Lord Harleston's affection, or certainly her own, she was obliged to remember her own circumstances with respect to the law. As she lay in bed that night, after pleading a headache and retiring early to ponder the situation, she finally acknowledged its truth.

"I do love him," she said aloud to the room. Indeed, she admitted, she had been loving him since the moment he first donned his groom's attire to assist her with her troubles. How wonderful it was to have complete confidence in the support of another! His manly attitude, the risks and discomforts he had already endured with no more than a laugh at the consequences, and *all for her*—it was more than she had ever been taught to expect from any man.

And she began to suspect now that his endeavours might have been somewhat the result, not of his duty to her father, but of his growing attachment to herself. She cringed at the thought of what might happen to him were he discovered to have taken part in this deception. The danger to Lady Mewhinny, as fearful as it was, was almost eclipsed by the possibility that Lord Harleston, a member of His Majesty's diplomatic corps, might be found to have assisted a fugitive from justice. And *she* had led him into it. Matters were becoming day by day more risky, as her immediate concern for Lady Mewhinny might lead to Lord Harleston's exposure.

"I shall have to give him up," Susan said to the nymphs playing on her ceiling. She could not look at them now without arousing the strangest and most delightful images of herself similarly engaged in the stable with Tom. But reason solemnly reminded her that he was not just Tom. He was Lord Harleston, and there could be no Lady Harleston with a stain such as hers on her reputation.

Suddenly it occurred to Susan that she did not even know his name. She loved him, she had even kissed him with abandon, and yet she did not know his Christian name.

"He will always be Tom to me," she told the nymphs, a tear rolling down her cheek. A fairy tale, no more.

Susan's thoughts kept her awake for hours, but matters never became any clearer. As hard as she tried to find a solution to their worries, the answer was still the same. She must expose Mr. Petworthy to the authorities. In the process it would be discovered that she was not Mrs. Faringdon and she would go to prison, perhaps to the gallows. As the hour increased, so did her morbidity and her overwrought mind lingered on this point. She imagined a moving scene in which she stood on the fatal platform and was asked, with the prospect of saving her life, just *who* had been her accomplice. She, of course, would refuse to answer and Lord Harleston, in the full stature of his nobility, would come forward to confess and save her. But she would deny it, and go to her fate.

As she pondered this depressing picture, the clock struck twelve and almost immediately there came a gentle tap at the door. Susan sat up in bed with a jerk and, uttering a joyous cry, ran to the door and flung it open. Tom stepped quickly into the room and took her into his arms.

For a moment her resolve was gone. Lord Harleston's coming had all the drama of a last-minute rescue from death. But she suddenly remembered herself and, determined to do what was right, drew back while gently removing his arms from about her. She dared not look into his eyes.

Tom released her and smiled. *She is so beautiful,* he thought. If only they were married already—but they were not. He did not know how he was to stand the wait, but until then he must respect her maidenly reserve. The circumstances were already so compromising, and his baroness should have nothing which could be whispered to her detriment. She had not called him here. It was only his fears for her comfort and his desire to be with her that had overcome his scruples and caused him to come.

He clasped his hands behind his back to avoid the impulse to take her in his arms again.

After clearing his throat, he explained himself. "I thought we must have a chance to talk as soon as possible after our experience of this afternoon." Then he added with a smile, "We were interrupted before we had a chance to plan what is to be done."

"Yes, we were," said Susan, her tone an involuntary show of regret. She was thinking it was the last time he would hold her thus, but Lord Harleston mistook her thoughts to be more in line with his own.

This reflection caused him to clear his throat again. "We must make a plan about what we will do for Lady Mewhinny," he said.

Susan nodded and sat down on the stool from her dressing table. Lord Harleston took the remaining chair. As soon as he was seated, Susan lifted her chin and gave him a direct look before saying, "I have been thinking it would be best if I went to the authorities and reported Mr. Petworthy's intentions. But I earnestly beg you, Lord Harleston, not to involve yourself in the matter. You may take the carriage and go on and I shall ask Vigor to accompany me."

"Nonsense," he said quite calmly, but giving her a look so loving that his remarks could not offend. "My dearest love, your brain is addled. Suppose you did go to the authorities, do you think they would not discover you are not who you say you are?" Susan lowered her eyes and stared at her hands in her lap, unwilling to admit that had been her intention. But he went on.

"And when, my love, they discover you are not who you pretend to be, do you think they will give any credence to your side of the matter? Mr. Petworthy will respond with indignation, and the matter will be dropped while they devote their energies to prosecuting you. And that I will not allow! Besides, Lady Mewhinny's activities appear distinctly peculiar to anyone who does not know her. The decision will not ride with you."

As he explained this to her in the most patient of voices, Susan's head came up and her eyes widened.

"I did not think of that," she admitted when he had finished.

"That is why you have me here to assist you," he said to tease her.

Susan looked at him with entreaty. "But then what shall we do?"

His mind went blank. She looked so lovely there, wrapped in her dressing gown, her hair about her shoulders. It was all he could do to remain in his seat.

Shaking the forbidden thoughts from his head, he quickly stood up and paced about the room, trying to keep his eyes from being drawn to her figure.

"Let us reflect for a moment," he said, thinking aloud. "What Petworthy intends to do is to get two unscrupulous justices of the peace to sign a warrant committing Lady Mewhinny to some sort of institution for the insane. And it will all hinge on the word of this Mr. Sodporth—who, I suspect, has little to recommend him other than his own self-praise. What we need, it would seem, is a means of discrediting this Sodporth fellow."

"But how are we to do it?" asked Susan eagerly.

His lordship pondered, but his love's presence had done much to diminish his powers of reasoning. "I could appear as myself," he ventured, "and run the scoundrels off."

"Oh, no, no, *no!*" cried Susan, horrified at the thought. She did not realize how she had parrotted the words of Mrs. Faringdon at the customs gate. "That would not do at all! They would be sure to recognize you in an instant and then we both should be ruined." She could not immediately understand why her remarks had brought a smile to his face.

"All right, madam," he said, pulling his forelock. "But you needn't strike me with your reticule this time. I acknowledge it was a foolish suggestion." As he reminded her of their adventure, a blush spread over her cheeks, and the look Tom gave her would have filled her with joy had it not torn her heart instead.

She waited in silence for his next idea, not trusting herself to speak.

He resumed, "If only my manservant were here, I should have a means of finding out something about Sodporth, or even Petworthy. *That* gentleman's actions would take on a different light if the exact details of his circumstances were known."

"Could you not send a message to your servant asking him to do those things for you?" Susan asked.

Lord Harleston shook his head. "He is not in London at the moment, and I am afraid that by the time a message could reach him too much time would be lost." He gave his full attention to the problem for a few minutes and then said with conviction, "What we need is our own medical man on the spot. If we could establish our own man down here at the inn in Heathfield, we could call on him whenever we wished. I could tell him to report to a Mrs. Faringdon up at the manor whenever he should be called. If he is in my employ he will not question my imposture, but I shall give him to understand that it was done in the interest of protecting Lady Mewhinny. And perhaps my man of business will have found something about Mr. Petworthy by then which will make him reluctant to pursue his scheme once it is proved to be known.''

He smiled at Susan regretfully. "However, it looks as if I shall have to fetch him myself.''

Susan's eyes lit up and she eagerly exclaimed, "That is an excellent plan! But there is no need for you to appear at all! You must simply engage a doctor, give him his instructions and send him to Heathfield. You might write to tell me when I can expect him." *She* had not been able to convince him to leave her, but his plan would make it necessary. He need not run any more risks.

"I shall do nothing of the kind." He spoke sternly. "Can you honestly believe, after today, that I would leave you to handle this alone?''

Susan's eyes beseeched him. "My lord, it is precisely because of today that you must not return. If you must satisfy yourself of my safety, send your groom. He may fetch the doctor just as well, and there will be no masquerade to explain. But I implore you, do not come back.''

He attempted to regain his humour. "Any more such declarations, madam, and I may begin to suspect you don't want me.''

Susan stamped her foot in frustration. "I will not be teased out of this again, my lord! I have tried to make myself clear on any number of occasions, but you always ... you make me laugh, or ...'' She dared not continue. She suspected he was well aware of his power to charm her. "You must stay in London. I will leave by post as soon as I am convinced that Lady Mewhinny is in no further danger." She did not add that she would never see him again.

Tom was staring at her intently. His lips were compressed in an uncompromising line, but all he said was "If I took the carriage, I could be in London by morning."

Susan's spirits rose at the thought of his being safely in London, but a dull pain possessed her chest.

"Of course you must," she said bravely. "It is the very best thing we could do for Lady Mewhinny. When Mr. Petworthy makes his accusations, I need only call for the doctor and he will give his opinion that nothing whatever is wrong with Lady Mewhinny's mind."

Lord Harleston nodded, only slightly worried that his own man would have doubts about her ladyship's sanity. But he would do his best to cast a favourable light on her peculiar occupations. Susan's other protests, he intended to ignore.

"Then I had better be off," he said. For an instant, Susan's face betrayed how sadly this affected her, but she quickly recovered enough to agree. Then, after standing and moving rapidly to the door, she opened it and looked up and down the hall to see if anyone was about. The hall was clear.

Holding the door open for him as if it were a shield between them, she whispered, "It is safe for you to go now, Lord Harleston."

He had followed her to the door and was looking at her strangely, but he did not remark on her coolness. After glancing once into the hall for his own satisfaction, he turned back, hoping perhaps for a more tender farewell. But Susan's extended hand was all that was offered.

He took it and held it firmly but gently until the warmth from his own removed its chill, and then he kissed it. He could almost feel the current which ran up her arm at the touch of his lips. Their eyes met, and he could not doubt his effect on her.

"Farewell, Mrs. Faringdon," he said in a whisper. "I shall return."

Susan grasped his hand involuntarily. "Oh, please, you mustn't," she said. "You must not do anything to harm yourself."

Buoyed up by her show of concern, he grinned as if he had not a fear in the world. "Just have a care to yourself and I shall be perfectly well," he promised.

Susan wanted desperately to argue with him further, but she was aware of the danger of keeping him standing in the hallway. She just had time to repeat her protest once more. Reluctantly then, she released him, and after another quick look to see if the way was clear, he departed for the stables.

CHAPTER ELEVEN

THE NEXT DAY, Susan made it known that she had sent Tom on to prepare her servants for her arrival. But, she said, she hoped to keep her ladyship company so long as there were two gentlemen to entertain. This remark made Mr. Petworthy regard her as if the possibility of her becoming an ally were stronger than he had thought.

However, Susan learned something else that morning which made her uneasy. It appeared that Vigor was gone. The servants were commenting upon his absence as if it were a strange occurrence indeed, but Lady Mewhinny said nothing about it. Susan wondered if she were even aware of his being gone, although certainly her ladyship seemed aware of most things that went on in her household. She also feared that the two gentlemen, suspecting the strong devotion of the faithful servant, might have disposed of him somehow before closing in on his mistress.

Mr. Sodporth's behaviour had undergone a serious alteration. He still regarded his food with the same attachment and savoured the pleasure of his port. But he had begun to wander about the house, turning up in the most disconcerting manner when least expected, and carrying about with him a small notebook. When found, he always looked up with that conspiratorial grin which Susan had learned to mistrust, but he would soon return to whatever he was noting in his book.

That evening Vigor returned in a hired carriage, bringing with him another visitor.

"My dear Susan," said Lady Mewhinny before dinner. "You must allow me to present to you an old friend of mine, Mr. Geoffrey Phillips."

He bowed and Susan extended her hand. Mr. Phillips was a young man by her ladyship's standards. He was perhaps sixty, with short grey hair worn in a serious cut. His clothes were well-fitting and without the least pretension to extravagance in fashion. His manner was formal, but in a pleasing way, and Susan took to him upon sight. The other two gentlemen, however, eyed him with a certain misgiving when he explained to the company at large that he was a solicitor from London.

"So kind of you to favour us with your company at this time of year," said Lady Mewhinny when they had all been seated. "Especially when there is so much to amuse one in London."

Mr. Phillips looked at her as if she had just paid him the greatest compliment. "My dear lady," he said. "You persist in thinking me the merest boy, when I assure you I have long held such revelry in abhorrence. You will have your guests thinking me the gayest of fellows."

She laughed and rapped his hand with her fan as if she knew better than to believe him. "Why, Mr. Phillips," she said, "if I have not grown too old to appreciate such customs, I am certain you have not." He blushed and looked highly gratified.

Susan was charmed by this little exchange, but Mr. Petworthy took the opportunity to twist it to his advantage. "You must forgive my aunt, Mr. Phillips," he said. "There are times when I do not think she realizes the advancement of her years. Of course," he added, when seeing the sudden frown on the face of his listener, "we must all envy her the tirelessness—one could almost say the *abnormal* level of her energy."

Mr. Phillips accepted this compliment to his hostess at its face value. "Tireless I believe she is, especially in the service of those creatures she styles her pensioners."

Mr. Petworthy laughed indulgently and was joined by the doctor. "So you are familiar with my aunt's little eccentricity," he said, bobbing his head and smiling. "Then you will perhaps not be surprised to learn that she devotes herself entirely to their care. It is a unique passion, one might almost say a *mania* with her."

Her ladyship's nephew, Susan reflected, might almost say *anything* if it would further the cause of his plot against his aunt. The matter was dropped. But as they dined, Mr. Phillips let fall a piece of news which interested all at the table.

"I have lately," he informed them, "been appointed justice of the peace in the next county."

Mr. Petworthy's head jerked up and he looked at his friend the doctor in alarm. His expression was not lost upon Susan, who rightly guessed that he feared his game was up. She blessed Providence, which had led Mr. Phillips to choose this time to make a visit, and her spirits were considerably lightened. Even Mr. Phillips's polite questions to herself did not impinge upon her sense of relief.

But after the ladies retired to the drawing room to take their tea, Susan experienced an increase of alarm. Lady Mewhinny chose that moment to sound Susan out as to her opinion on an expansion of the Society's purpose. She proposed enlarging the scope of its protection to extend to all wild beasts brought into England. The wild beast booth at the fair was what gave her the idea, she explained, for there she had seen offered for sale both a camel and a hyena.

"And what anyone could possibly want with a hyena in the garden and to what good purpose, I cannot imagine," she said indignantly. "A camel has its uses, to be sure, but I find it hard to believe that a gentleman would prefer a camel to a horse on the downs or in town. Its paces could not be superior. I think something must be done to rescue beasts who are taken as mere curiosities and then tired of. Do you not agree, Susan?"

Susan was afraid to give an answer for fear of encouraging her ladyship to speak of the matter again in front of the gentlemen. But neither could she disappoint her friend.

"But, Kitty," she said finally, "'Ow would such a s'ing be accomplished? Surely you could not keep zem all 'ere?"

Lady Mewhinny's delighted laugh filled the room. "My dear Susan, how absurd! Of course, I would not bring them here. Can you imagine a herd of camels in the park? They would be certain to get into the vegetable garden and upset the cook! No. I intend sending them back where they came from!"

Susan's mind whirled at the thought of the vast sums that would be required to accomplish this, but she had no chance to reply before the ladies were joined by Mr. Phillips.

"I have decided to precede the other gentlemen," he explained, "for I have little taste for port. A cup of tea would suit me nicely, yes. Thank you, Mrs. Faringdon."

Susan poured him a cup from the tray and then excused herself, saying she must run up to her room for a warmer shawl. In reality, she meant to use the chance to eavesdrop on the other two gentlemen. Their plans would now require a change, and she hoped to find out what this would be.

She found the dining room door to the hall ajar and no footman was there to observe her queer behaviour. After approaching the door on tiptoe, she placed her ear close to the opening and heard the conversation that followed.

Mr. Sodporth was entreating his friend. "Might not this Phillips fellow agree to supply the second signature, my dear Petworthy? If he is a justice of the peace, he must certainly be called on to do these things. And newly appointed as he is, his experience will be slight.''

Mr. Petworthy seemed much struck by the suggestion. "It is possible," he said after a long pause. "Yes! Sodporth, you are a genius! Perhaps all is not lost, as I had feared. But we must proceed cautiously! He is a friend of hers, after all. And the suggestion must not come from me." Susan could imagine him vigorously shaking his head. "By no means. *You* must supply him with both the idea and the proof. As a medical man, your superior knowledge of such matters must be relied upon. Yes, that's it. You must endeavour to convince him that separating her from her fortune and Society would be the very best thing for her. And he must not be made to fear she would be placed in a lunatic asylum. She might be as closely guarded here. And I *do* feel," he added, as though suddenly caught by a scruple, "that she might be kept comfortably here. There is the whole wing now occupied by the monkeys." He ended with a snicker.

Susan was horrified anew. Mr. Petworthy, it seemed, was not to be deterred. The very presence of Mr. Phillips, which she had hoped would be his undoing, was going to be a means of hastening his evil purpose. The sounds of chairs scraping the floor awoke her to her own danger, and she fled noiselessly up the staircase in her light slippers.

Upstairs in her room, she paused to catch her breath and reflect. If only Tom were here, she thought. But she must not let herself think of him again, for she was resolved not to involve him further. He had said he would return, and she believed he meant it. Part of her desperately wanted him to come back, to know that he loved her enough to put himself at risk. If he did not, she would suffer the disappointment of knowing he had cared for her no more than had her father. The possibility of a similarity between the two situations was almost more than Susan could bear.

But this was entirely different, she reminded herself. If Lord Harleston were to come back, he would be in peril of being discovered. The thought filled her with fear. If he returned, she would have to try to persuade him to keep out of Lady Mewhinny's troubled affairs. But there would be nothing she could do to stop him. He would make his own decision, and would not be directed by her. Until she knew, however, she must deal with the matter of Mr. Petworthy's latest change of plans. She must be firm and deal with this new development on her own.

A little more thought and Susan knew what she must do. She must engage Mr. Phillips's attention as much as possible while he was there. Lady Mewhinny, she supposed, would be occupied as usual with her charges and could not be depended upon to keep him company. She herself must be the one to keep the gentlemen apart.

Hastily then, she grabbed the woollen shawl which had been her pretext for leaving the room and hurried down to the drawing room to join the others. And it was fortunate she did, she soon saw, for Lady Mewhinny had most unwisely left the gentlemen to themselves. Mr. Sodporth was at that moment regaling Mr. Phillips with some of his most extreme cases.

Mr. Petworthy, on the other hand, was most uncharacteristically engaged in reading a book, or so it appeared. Upon seeing her, however, he closed it and stood to welcome her to the room. Indicating a chair rather closer to himself than to the others he opened with these words, "Ah, Mrs. Faringdon. You have come to join us. We had almost feared you did not mean to come back. You will not object, I hope, to an all-male company?"

If he had meant to discourage her with these words, Susan did not take the hint, but felt obliged still to take the chair he offered her, even though it was farther away from Mr. Phillips than she could have wished. That gentleman smiled as she entered, but gave his attention immediately back to Mr. Sodporth, who continued to display his knowledge and competence.

"You must forgive my friend, Mrs. Faringdon," said Mr. Petworthy by way of explanation, "but his professional interest is so consuming that he quite naturally prefers to discuss it. I cannot suppose such matters interest you, however, and I flatter myself that you will not object to *my* conversation."

Susan gave him a look which, she hoped, expressed cold, but polite acquiescence, but she wished he would not always forestall her objections so thoroughly. She was not pleased to be trapped in such close conversation with her adversary, and she kept her replies to his sallies a simple monotone.

Whenever an opportunity came to draw the others into their tête-à-tête, she took it, no matter how flimsy the opening. She hoped she merely gave the impression that it did not suit her sense of propriety to be monopolized by one gentleman's conversation, but there were times when even Mr. Phillips regarded her oddly. It was an exhausting evening, but true to her purpose, she remained with the others, diverting the solicitor's attention whenever she could, until he rose for bed. Then, she, too, stood up, bade good-night to the others and made gratefully for her room.

Susan was so done in by her efforts that she had no difficulty in achieving sleep. Not even her worries over Lord Harleston's return could keep her awake. As her eyes closed for the last time, she only hoped, for his sake, that his good sense had overcome his scruples, and that he would see the wisdom of her request. Surely, once away from her, he would know how right she was.

Susan slept soundly and found to her horror upon awakening that the morning had passed and it was already afternoon. She dressed in a hurry and went downstairs, only to find the breakfast parlour deserted. A servant detained her by insisting in the kindest way upon bringing her something to eat, so it was much later than she could have wished that she was able to join the gentlemen. When she finally found them, she perceived that Mr. Phillips and Mr. Sodporth had been enjoying a quiet tête-à-tête for some time in the library. Mr. Petworthy was nowhere in sight.

Mr. Sodporth was speaking in a low, cautious voice, which boded no good, and Susan heard references to "monomania" and "chronic dementia." Her entrance into the room provided an interruption, however, in that Mr. Phillips's excellent manners would not allow the conversation to exclude her.

After greeting her soberly, he invited her to join them, against the concealed wishes of his companion. Mr. Sodporth was confident enough of his success, however, that he agreed to her presence without being put off his subject.

"Mrs. Faringdon," he addressed her, "Mr. Phillips and I have just been discussing the preferred treatment for a condition known as 'monomania without paralysis.' I was just telling him what I have found to be most effective in its treatment."

"Pray, do not let me interrupt you," said Susan, taking a chair between them. "You must go on, by all means. I am certain to find it interesting." The light of battle was in her eyes.

Mr. Phillips briefly directed an enquiring look at her before seating himself and preparing to listen with gravity.

"In such cases," began Mr. Sodporth with a confident air, "complete removal from society is most earnestly advised. Illusions of grandeur, which frequently accompany the disease, might then be avoided. A strict regimen, tartar emetics and, ahem— (he coughed slightly with an apologetic glance at Susan)—the reestablishment of suppressed evacuations are the recommended course of treatment."

"Would a course of sea baths be beneficial?" asked the solicitor.

Mr. Sodporth shook his head. "I fear not," he said. "In those cases in which sea baths or trips to mineral springs are recommended, the purpose is for one thing only—the complete cessation of busyness. That is most essential. I find the reiterated application of leeches to absorb the fluid effused in the brain to be *much* more effective. That, along with certain medications, will effect a cure more certainly than courses of mild exercise."

"You do not believe in the benefits of exercise to an afflicted mind?"

Mr. Sodporth shook his head again with an air of indulgence toward a pupil. "No, my dear sir. I cannot pretend that I do. Oh, perhaps, during a walk, particularly in the springtime when nature is grand, a patient might be momentarily diverted from her delusions, but not for long. Labour, I should say, would procure a more salutary diversion."

Susan was growing more and more alarmed as the conversation progressed. She could not tell whether Mr. Sodporth had already broached the subject of Lady Mewhinny's lunacy to her guest or whether the discussion was purely a general one. Mr. Phillips's grave air suggested that it *had* been mentioned, but until she was certain she dared not venture an opinion for fear of precipitating a crisis.

The gentlemen went on discussing the proper medication for chronic dementia, and the list, which included belladonna, hemlock, purgatives and tartar emetics, frightened her as much as a subsequent discussion about electric treatments and galvanism. She was about to make an attempt to divert the conversation to another topic, when Mr. Phillips turned toward her suddenly and posed a question.

"And do you agree, Mrs. Faringdon, that our hostess has been exhibiting an irregularity of mind?"

The question stunned her, both by its suddenness and by the manner in which it was asked, for Mr. Phillips seemed in complete earnest. His manner was consistent with one who was painfully awaiting confirmation. A glance at Mr. Sodporth showed how satisfied that gentleman was with his achievement, and he smiled at her in a way that was distinctly threatening.

But Susan did not quail. After an initial silence, she straightened her shoulders and spoke bravely.

"*Non!* I most emphatically do not, Mr. Phillips! I s'ink Lady Mewhinny is ze kindest, most considerate creature I 'ave ever met. And I find nos'ing at all irregular in 'er be'aviour."

He looked at her strangely. Mr. Sodporth's eyes were like daggers, but he made funny little noises as though her opinion, though touching, was not to be considered in the matter.

"Then you do not fear," persisted Mr. Phillips, "that all her attention to the monkeys, admittedly unusual as it is, might be a symptom of a mental aberration?"

Susan ignored Mr. Sodporth's attempt to remonstrate and answered firmly, "*Non, monsieur,* I do not. I s'ink it more a symptom of 'er kind 'eart."

He did not reply to her comment, but instead turned to face the doctor. "What have you to say to that, Sodporth?"

Mr. Sodporth had by this time decided on his choice of tactics and showed no outward distress. He shook his head with a pathetic little smile. "I think Mrs. Faringdon's opinion reflects her own benevolence, but I cannot allow her to have the same experience in such matters as myself. Often the subjects of my examinations are so convincing in their mania that lay persons might not perceive the danger to the subjects themselves. And I flatter myself that it is concern for those same subjects which leads me to take action in such cases—often over the protests of their relatives. It is a grievous business, as you can see, but I always put the patient's interest first.

"Indeed," he went on with an embarrassed laugh, "it was the purest accident which caused me to be here, an invitation from my dear friend Petworthy to keep him company while he rusticated a bit. Once here, however, I could not help making certain professional observations. And when I first mentioned them to Petworthy, you may imagine his distress. The poor fellow was sorely grieved—almost undone!" He shook his head again with palpable sadness. Susan wondered that she had ever mistaken his smiles for evidence of cordiality. The man was as devious as a fox.

Throughout this sad explanation, Mr. Phillips had said nothing, nor did he now venture an opinion. Instead, he rose and excused himself, saying he had letters to write before the day was gone. Susan rose with him, unwilling to be caught in the room alone with Mr. Sodporth. Once out in the corridor she would gladly have repeated for him her testament of faith in Lady Mewhinny, but Bates appeared immediately and desired Mr. Phillips to wait on her ladyship in her study. He bowed to Susan, still looking grave, and disappeared down the hall.

The day dragged on, and Susan could not help making many trips to the window at the slightest sound, to see whether it was Tom returning from London. He had not given her any idea about when to expect the doctor's arrival in Heathfield. But imagining all he must do in order to find a medical man willing to kick his heels in a country inn for an indefinite time, she did not really expect results that day. She wondered, in fact, that she had agreed to the scheme, for she now perceived it as impossible. Susan did not realize the power of persuasion at his lordship's disposal as a peer, and that if he chose he would be able to gather an army of doctors at his command.

She prayed fervently, however, to receive a note soon, both advising her of the doctor's arrival and assuring her of Lord Harleston's safety.

At dinner that evening her nerves were further upset by a new direction in Mr. Petworthy's attention to herself. She had no doubt that the sum of her remarks that afternoon had been relayed to him by his friend. Now he knew her to be an enemy, and seeing that his plan was in the balance, chose to take an offensive tack.

"You must allow me to compliment you, Mrs. Faringdon," he said, "on the rapid improvement in your English since I arrived." The remark was made with a suggestion of incredulity. Mr. Phillips, she saw, took an immediate interest in the conversation.

Vowing not to volunteer any more information than was necessary, she replied, "S'ank you," and stopped. But her silence did not deter him.

"Indeed," he continued, "there has been *such* an improvement that I wonder if you had not had some prior knowledge of the language." He clearly suspected her, but Susan was so angered by his tone as to override any feelings of fear.

She smiled tightly. "As you must recall, Monsieur Petworz'y, my late 'usband was Eenglish, and it was in Eenglish zat we conversed. It is only when I am just returned from France, as I was quite recently, zat I forget certain words. Zat may per'aps account for it."

"Perhaps so," he said, also smiling. "For my man has spoken to your maid and she said you hardly spoke a word of English when you took her on. In Calais, I believe?"

Susan nodded coldly. *Peg again,* she thought. Is this what she's been spending her time doing, talking of me to Mr. Petworthy's servant to confirm his suspicions?

He was hardly smiling now. The look in his eyes was a little frightening. "And I understand you engaged

her and then did not require her services until the boat
was ready to sail.''

Susan thought frantically for a moment. Angry
though she was, she could not help fearing the end of
his questions. ''I was misinformed,'' she told him finally, ''about ze level of 'er attainments.'' Wryly she
told herself this was almost the case. ''You see, ze girl
'ad been turned off by 'er last employers and needed
a post. I was in need of a maid, my own 'aving elected
to stay in France. I s'ought it should serve. But as soon
as I get to London, I intend to turn 'er off. She 'as not
been satisfactory.''

At this Lady Mewhinny's voice piped in, ''I am so
glad to hear you say that, Susan dear. I did not like to
suggest it, but the girl is sadly lacking. Her behaviour
belowstairs is quite deplorable, they tell me, and I did
wonder if you were absolutely right to engage her. But
it is charitable of you to carry her as far as London.
There, certainly, she will be able to find work that suits
her better.'' And with that she smiled wickedly and
gave Susan a wink, which shocked her considerably.

But the gentlemen did not appear to notice. Mr.
Sodporth was devoting his entire attention to his meal,
perhaps feeling that his work was done. Mr. Petworthy was intent upon discrediting Susan in some fashion, and Mr. Phillips was listening attentively to the
conversation between them. Susan could only wonder what he made of it.

But Mr. Petworthy was chuckling indulgently.
''That is another matter altogether, Auntie dear. How

your mind does wander! I was only making the point that the girl's description of her employer in Calais was so very different from the lady in our company that one might almost wonder if...*they were the same person!*'' This was said with an air of innocence, but with such emphasis as to be nearly an accusation.

It was so outlandish and farfetched, however, that Susan could not help but laugh. Mr. Petworthy's case was not furthered by her spontaneity.

''Zat is quite amusing, Monsieur Petworz'y,'' she said. ''But I can assure you—most regretfully, I might add—zat I am indeed ze same person who engaged Peg in Calais.''

He retired, defeated for the moment, but later in the evening resumed his questions. He enquired of Mr. Phillips if he were not fluent in French and if he might not like to oblige Mrs. Faringdon with a conversation in her native tongue. This she denied, indicating a wish not to exclude her hostess, who spoke none at all. Fortunately, Lady Mewhinny did not press her to indulge herself, which Susan attributed to her ladyship's sense of propriety. Surely it was an improper suggestion that two members of a party should indulge in a private conversation to the exclusion of others.

Once Mr. Petworthy tried to catch her out on her husband's name, stating quite innocently that he was certain she had called him James and not John. But Susan replied confidently that she had never had occasion to mention her husband's Christian name before, so he must be mistaken.

It was attempts like these, however, which finally persuaded her to seek her bed early that evening. The necessity of always being on her toes was exhausting. But she took comfort from the knowledge that, for the moment at least, Tom was safely removed from her difficulties.

CHAPTER TWELVE

THE NEXT MORNING, Susan descended the stairs rather late again. This time she did it on purpose, for she realized that if she were discovered in her masquerade she could do nothing whatsoever to help Lady Mewhinny. It was better to avoid Mr. Petworthy's questions, she reflected, than to risk being ejected from the house before she could be useful.

Later emerging from the breakfast parlour alone, however, she heard the sound of voices emanating from the drawing room. She approached the door quietly and listened, but the door was so thick that all she could hear at first was a faint mumbling. Then suddenly a voice was raised, and she was certain she heard Mr. Sodporth announcing his theories with great emphasis.

Good God! she thought. He was denouncing her now! She did not doubt that Mr. Petworthy was with him and she feared that Mr. Phillips was also there, fully taken in. In defiance of all the rules of etiquette, she was about to burst in upon them and defend Lady Mewhinny's sanity, when the sound of coach wheels stopped her. It was Tom!

Immediately she let go the door handle. Her emotions pulled at her from every direction. If Tom had brought a doctor with him, it might solve the present crisis. Her own protestations, she knew, would sound weak compared to the strength of the doctor's arguments, and her emotional defense of Lady Mewhinny would serve for nothing. But Tom! Her heart filled with anguish. What might happen to Lord Harleston if he should be discovered somehow in the confusion? He did love her. He had come back. But she must run quickly to warn him. She must beg him to go back to the inn to notify the doctor that he was needed at once. But she hoped to be able to persuade Tom not to return with him.

Susan did not perceive as she headed to the stables that Mr. Petworthy was following her. He had watched her from a curtained window in the corridor where he awaited the outcome of the discussion in the drawing room. And her suspicious behaviour led him to believe there was something he could turn to his advantage—to remove, in fact, the sole obstacle to his plan.

With a quickening heart, Susan opened the stable door and flew in. There was Tom, rubbing down the horses with straw, but as soon as he heard her he turned and came striding forward with open arms. However, something in her hurried manner must have alerted him to her distress, for instead of taking her in his arms he took her hands and said, "My dearest love! What is it?"

Susan looked down, unable to witness the love in his eyes without responding to it. "Lord Harleston," she said, in a voice deliberately made to sound cool, "I am afraid you must summon your medical man at once— if you have brought one with you. There is not a moment to lose."

But his lordship did not depart immediately. Instead he gently lifted her chin with his hand and said, "Of course I will. He is in Heathfield and I can fetch him in an instant. But why the formality, my love? What has happened?"

Susan's defenses were considerably weakened by this entreaty. Tears of confusion sprang to her eyes. "You ought not to have come back," she said, allowing him to take her into his arms and, with contradictory logic, throwing her arms about his neck. "You ought not to be taking such a risk."

But before she could send him away, Mr. Petworthy stepped forward and spoke with a sneer. "So! It's my Lord Harleston, is it? And what kind of indecent deception is this? I suspected you from the first, my girl. Weaseling your way into my aunt's affections to get her fortune. I knew it! But I had no idea you had a lover for accomplice!"

At Mr. Petworthy's first word, Lord Harleston had whirled round and placed himself between Susan and her accuser. Now he had had enough. Before the villain could speak again, he sprang at him and floored him with one blow. Then, as Lady Mewhinny's nephew whimpered and begged for mercy, he lifted him into the air by the collar of his coat and demanded an apology.

Vigor, who had entered during the scuffle and watched silently for a moment, cleared his throat and made them a bow. "If you please, madam," he said to Susan. "Lady Mewhinny told me to ask you and Mr. Petworthy to join her in the drawing room." His face was impassive. For all he gave away he might as easily have been witnessing a conversation taking place between a groom and her ladyship's nephew on the finer points of a horse.

Tom had recovered his temper by now and released Mr. Petworthy without ceremony. That gentleman, relieved to have been saved from worse treatment, made sure he was out of reach of Tom's powerful arms before straightening his frock coat and cravat. "You shall answer for your impudence!" he tossed back over his shoulder. "My aunt shall hear of this imposture!"

Tom moved to Susan's side and took her arm to lead her into the house, but she shook herself free. Vigor, although waiting for her, did not seem to be listening. "No, my lord," she told Tom in an angry whisper "She did not ask for you. This is my doing and I shall go alone."

He started to protest, but she silenced him. She had pled with him enough; now it was time to be firm. "No. Please. It will be much worse for me—I promise—if we are both exposed in front of the others. Let me do what I can to help Lady Mewhinny. I am afraid it is too late for anything else." Then, seeing that her anger had wounded him, she gave him a wistful smile and lifted her skirts to step through the straw. Anxiously, he watched her join Vigor and disappear out the door.

With a heavy heart Susan followed Mr. Petworthy into the drawing room. Now that he was out of sight of Lord Harleston, the villain felt quite safe in resuming an air of righteous indignation and he threw her a look of triumph as he crossed the threshold. Inside the company was assembled.

Lady Mewhinny, who was seated by the fire doing her needlework, greeted them with her customary serenity. "Ah, there you are, my dear," she said to Susan. "And Augustus! It might interest you to know what's been going on during your absence."

Susan saw the grim look on Mr. Phillips's face and she feared the worst. Holding back tears, she made one final effort to save her friend. "Mr. Phillips, please," she begged, abandoning her false accent in her sincerity. "You must not listen to these men. They are doing her ladyship a terrible injustice. It was all planned!"

Much to her surprise, he smiled. "You need have no fears for her ladyship, Mrs. Faringdon. I can assure you she was fully aware of their plan. That was why she sent Vigor to fetch me, you see. She has been expecting something like this any time this past year."

Susan looked round and finally saw Mr. Sodporth. He was cowering on a chair in the corner, looking as if all the stuffing had been knocked out of him. "Then

you are not going to sign the commitment papers?"
she asked Mr. Phillips.

"No, he is not, my dear," said Lady Mewhinny
calmly. "Augustus, I have 'rumbled your lay,' as you
would undoubtedly put it yourself when you are mix-
ing with your usual company. We shall see just who
gets packing and to where!"

Mr. Petworthy had turned deathly pale. "But,
Auntie!" he protested. "I cannot think what you
mean! I have acted with the purest motives. Why, I
was just coming to inform you of the grossest deception going on right under your own roof. It concerns
this Mrs. Faringdon and—*my lord*." He spoke the last
two words in a withering manner that made Susan
cringe with guilt.

But Lady Mewhinny intervened. "If you mean Lord
Tom," she said quite tranquilly, "I know all about
him. And I would rather not hear another word on the
subject, thank you. You should know by now, Augustus, that very little goes on under my roof, as you
put it, that I do not know. I have been very grateful for
Susan's company while I was waiting for Mr. Phillips
to arrive. She has been good protection for me from
you and your accomplice. Although naturally, my
dear," she said, turning once again to Susan, "I would
not have kept you here against your will just for that."

Susan was speechless with shock. Lady Mewhinny
knew all about Lord Harleston? And yet she had said
nothing about it? Then she must have known about
her own misdoings as well. The thought filled Susan
with shame for her deception and gratitude for her

ladyship's forbearance. She had cut her nephew off and refused to hear him on the subject.

Mr. Petworthy was similarly surprised, although he had not done with his blustering. He continued to protest his innocence, divorcing himself from the actions of his friend and insisting that if Sodporth were mistaken in his diagnosis no one would be more relieved than he. Mr. Phillips judged it was time to step in.

"Nonsense!" he said, to put an end to the business. "You have schemed to do away with your aunt and to obtain her fortune. I have had you followed these many months, Petworthy, and it is clear that you have been trading on expectations of these events for some time. It is known throughout the city that you are all done up. You have massive debts and, it is reasonably assumed, were involved in a recent scandal in which a widow was cheated out of her fortune. You had best give up the sham, Petworthy, if you do not wish to have the full story disclosed before a court."

The result of this speech was that Petworthy, who had turned first red with indignation, then rather greenish, was left without a word. He fell back into a chair and placed his head in his hands.

Lady Mewhinny glanced briefly at him without lifting her head from her work. Then she resumed and said in a tolerant voice, "You always did remind me of my sister-in-law, Augustus. And she never could be relied upon to tell the truth. There was bad blood in the Mewhinnys. What a mercy Sir William was spared any of it."

Then she went on, "But I hope you do not think I will allow a nephew of Sir William's to languish in a prison cell, no matter how well he deserves it. Mr. Phillips has arranged to pay back whatever of your debts are owed to honourable persons, particularly the widow, Augustus." Here her voice was almost stern. "The remainder I shall leave unpaid to teach them not to do business with you again. And," she added forcibly, "to keep you ever in their minds should you try to enter the country again."

Mr. Petworthy looked up at this with a degree of hope. "You will assist me in getting out of the country?" he asked.

Her ladyship nodded. "It is more than you deserve, of course, and a great burden to be placing on the French, despite their excesses. But I cannot have you lurking about England, for I make no mistake you would murder me in my bed if you could." This was all said quite calmly, and she added a particular afternote to Susan, "I hope you will forgive me for sending him there, dear."

Her remark puzzled Susan. Why should Lady Mewhinny apologize to Susan for sending her nephew to France if she already knew Susan was not French? But it was no time to ask for enlightenment. She was pleased to see that Lady Mewhinny did not think her beneath reproach for her own deception. Mr. Phillips then made the suggestion that Susan should be allowed to retire while the others discussed the arrangements which were to be made. This included Mr. Petworthy's signature on a document, which had already been prepared, renouncing all further claim to his uncle's estate after the death of his aunt. Susan left the room and went up to her chamber.

Now she knew it was time to leave. They had been discovered. Susan had only to find out what action Mr. Phillips or Lady Mewhinny planned to take with respect to her misdeeds. With a perverse calm, she packed her bags and sent word to the stables that they would leave on the morrow. She thought it would be best not to face Lord Harleston until then. For herself, she was resigned to whatever was in store for her. But the problem of Lord Harleston's stubbornness remained. How could she protect him now and convince him to abandon her to her fate? She spent the remainder of the day trying to form an argument that would serve.

Uncertain of her reception, she nevertheless went down to dinner at the appropriate time. She found Lady Mewhinny and Mr. Phillips seated comfortably together, and they greeted her as though nothing had happened. They explained, very calmly, that the other gentlemen had departed, but nothing further was said on the subject until Lady Mewhinny and she rose from the table and made their way into the drawing room.

Once they were alone together, Lady Mewhinny gave Susan some startling news. "Dear Susan, I must tell you that your maid has also departed."

Susan looked at her in blank astonishment. "Peg?" she asked, thoroughly dumbfounded. She had forgotten all about her.

"Yes, my dear," said Lady Mewhinny, only mildly apologetic. "Perhaps I ought to have consulted you, but I really did it for the best. You see, when I saw that she was forming an attachment for my nephew Augustus's manservant, I thought it might be an answer to a dilemma. The man is not a good sort, but I truly believe he had nothing to do with Augustus's plans, and considering this, I gave him a few coins and dropped a word in his ear. He was most anxious to take himself off before there could be any trouble. And I do not think he was loath to take the girl with him."

"But why, Lady Mewhinny?" asked Susan, still confused. "I admit I will not miss the girl at all, but why did you think it needed to be done?"

Lady Mewhinny positively giggled and gave her a sly look, "Why, my dear, let us just say I did not approve of her behaviour and thought you would do better with another maid. Before Augustus's man came, you know, she was forever making eyes at your groom."

Susan blushed to the roots of her hair. The implication was unmistakable. Now that the subject had been broached, however, she felt she must make an apology.

"Oh, Kitty," she said earnestly. "I hope you will forgive me. Indeed, it was all my doing and I was fully conscious of the injustice to you in the deception. So conscious that I was eager to be off in spite of the kindness you have shown me. I will never forget it," she said, a catch in her throat. "But we felt we had to stay on to do something to stop Mr. Petworthy from harming you. And Lord—Lord Tom, that is,'' she amended, hoping to keep his name at least out of their discussion, ''he was only doing it to assist me.''

''I know it, my dear,'' said Lady Mewhinny kindly, dismissing the rest with a wave of her hand. ''And believe me, I am most grateful. And I, in turn, shall apologize for Mr. Phillips's questioning you. He told me he thought he should assure himself of your good intentions. But I expect you will wish to be getting on with your journey.''

Susan could only nod in silence, but as Mr. Phillips chose that moment to join them, she excused herself with the notion of packing and went up to her room. As she lay that night, looking up at the nymphs on the ceiling, she could only wonder at her ladyship's perspicacity, that she should have found them all out without the least trouble at all.

Susan tried not to think about her final meeting with Tom on the morrow. It appeared that she had been spared by Lady Mewhinny's great sense of mercy, but she had nearly led Tom to his ruin. Tomorrow she would have to send him away from her for good. But in spite of her firm resolution, she spent the better part of the night dreading what was to come.

THE NEXT MORNING, bright and early, Susan prepared to leave. The coach was at the door, Tom standing beside it at attention. As the light from the sun struck the whiteness in his hair, Susan felt a dull pain rise in her throat, but she steeled her resolution and went into the drawing room to bid Lady Mewhinny goodbye.

Her ladyship was alone for the moment, and as Susan entered she beckoned her to the chair beside her.

"There is just one more thing I want to say to you before you go, dearest Susan," she said. "And I hope you will not be offended to hear it from me."

Susan hastened to reassure her. "Of course not! How could I be, Kitty, after your kindness to me! What is it?"

Her ladyship smiled at her wisely and patted her hand. "Just this, dear. I would advise you to use a little more discretion when having an affair with your groom. If Augustus, silly and stupid as he is, could discover you, there will surely be others who will do so. And they might not be so easily silenced." She delivered this statement with the greatest calm.

"An affair with my groom?" Susan could do nothing more than repeat the words in bewilderment.

Lady Mewhinny patted her hand again. "Of course, my dear. Did you not hear me say I knew all about it? But I would not let Augustus expose you publicly, cad that he is! And you must not fear I disapprove of you. No, no! It is not that. Why, I took Vigor to my bed not long after Sir William's death, so I understand perfectly, but it is easier to be discreet in one's own house than in strange surroundings. I just thought I should drop a word in your ear."

"You took Vigor to your—" Susan stopped herself before her own astonishment could give her away. Lady Mewhinny had not discovered the imposture after all. Susan remembered that Mr. Petworthy had not actually used Lord Harleston's name once in the drawing room. When he had referred so scathingly to "my lord," Lady Mewhinny must have thought he was referring to her groom's nickname. A wave of relief rushed through her as she thanked Providence that she had not used his name herself, and that her ladyship's deafness to her accent had made her oblivious to its absence.

Blushing furiously, Susan gulped and thanked Lady Mewhinny for her advice.

"And there is one more thing, my dear," said her ladyship. "I understand that your fortune is not in your hands, but I would so like you to become a member of our Society. I would gladly enter your name as an honorary member, if you have no objection. There are so many ways you might be helpful to us, and I feel your gentle heart is worth more to our cause than any amount of donations."

Susan thanked her warmly and accepted the honour, giving her governess's address as her own. Then she rose and did her best to conceal her agitation while they made their affectionate goodbyes, after which she walked in a daze to the carriage.

In another minute she and Tom were bowling down the road at an eager pace and the last bit of Sussex was soon out of sight. She was hardly recovered from her shock, when the carriage drew over to the side of the road and came to an abrupt stop. In another second, Lord Harleston had opened the door and joined her inside.

He took her in his arms and kissed her ruthlessly before asking, "What happened, Susan? How was it all resolved?"

She answered him in a daze, which had not been lessened by his lordship's embrace, "She knew it. Kitty had discovered it all. And she had hired Mr. Phillips to handle the matter before we even knew what was wrong." She looked up at Tom and saw that his eyes were lit with admiration.

"Had she, by God! What a sharp-witted old woman! I can see that I wronged her. But what about you, love? Did she say nothing about you?"

Susan forgot her resolution. "Oh, Tom!" she said. "She thought I was having an affair with my groom! I thought she had discovered us as well. I had even dropped my French accent. But she thought we were..." She trailed off, aware of the danger of completing her sentence, and blushed.

Lord Tom threw his head back and laughed. "What a perfect idea!" he said finally. "I wonder we did not think of it ourselves! We must invite her ladyship to the wedding."

But here Susan recalled her determination. "There must be no wedding, my lord. You forget. I am sure, upon reflection, that you will see the wisdom of it. Why, we are practically strangers."

"Strangers!" He almost released her in his surprise. "But how can you say that? Why, madam, need I remind you that you have made use—very freely and frequently I might add—of my Christian name!"

Susan looked at him indignantly. "I have not!" she replied. "That was purely a masquerade!"

He gazed down at her lovingly and shook his head. With sudden comprehension she weakened and her eyes misted over. "Are you really Tom?" she asked him, reaching a soft hand up to touch his cheek.

That was more than his lordship could resist, and he assured her with all the force of his kisses that it was indeed so.

Drawing back at last, with all the courage she could muster, Susan made one last attempt. "Lord Harleston, you forget yourself. I am grateful... more than grateful for all you have done to help me. But we must not deceive ourselves. You must leave me at the next town and I will go on by post from there. You needn't worry about me; I shall be perfectly all right."

He laughed at her seriousness and tried to bring her into his arms again, but Susan resisted. "I'm afraid it is much too late for that with me," he said. "I love you. And you love me!"

Susan threw him a look of anguish. "But what if they send me to gaol? What if they hang me?"

He shook his head and forced her to rest within the confines of his arms. With resignation, she gave up pretending.

"It will not do, my love," she sighed. "I will not be Lady Harleston with the legal authorities after me. You would be ruined and I would rather die."

Ignoring this protest completely, he answered, "Then imagine me, if you will, Susan—old and weary, as I someday shall be. And alone. Absolutely alone. For I will have no other.''

Her eyes filled with tears again before she understood his tactics. Then, perceiving a twinkle behind his tragic demeanour, she tried to hold him off, laughing reluctantly through her tears.

But soon the realization of her own weakness stirred her to anger. ''It will not serve, my lord! You may try to break my heart, but you shall not break my resolve. I know what I must do. And marry you I will not!''

''Not even if your name should be cleared?'' he whispered into her hair.

The warmth of his breath sent a delicious chill down to her toes and she wanted to melt against him. ''Please do not tease me,'' she said in a small voice.

He took her chin in his hand and made her look up at him. ''I am not teasing. One of the things I did in London was to work toward obtaining your pardon. I have already arranged for an audience with Prinny. His aides tell me he is very receptive to the notion, and my application will be a mere formality. He had quite an admiration for your father. And besides, he is such a romantic that he will not be able to refuse me when I tell him how much I love you. Of course, he will want to be invited to the wedding.'' Susan opened her mouth to protest again, but he silenced her by placing a finger on her lips. ''I will simply tell him I made your acquaintance in Calais. He need not know anything about this adventure.''

She shook herself free. "My lord, I know you mean to do as you say. But how can you be certain of anything? I am not such a goose that I do not know how fickle the Regent can be. By the time you get back to London, he will have forgotten his intentions of yesterday."

It was Lord Harleston's turn to shake his head. For once he regarded her in perfect seriousness. "No, he will not." He reached into his pocket and pulled out an official-looking document. "Unpredictable though he may be at times, even the Regent cannot ignore a commitment to a peer. I have an appointment to see him, and I shall not give up until I have your pardon." Then he added, "But in truth, Susan, you mistake the seriousness of it. Your father knew it would all blow over. He said as much to me. And I have no doubt he had his suspicions on another score."

Startled, Susan looked up at him with big eyes.

He nodded. Then, his expression softening, he said, "Do you think he did not wish for this match? He must have known I had only to see you and know your courageous heart before falling instantly in love with you. Oh, perhaps he could not be certain," he said, when he saw the lingering doubt on her face. "But he must have seen from the outset that things were going as he wished. I know I saw it myself."

Susan gazed into his sparkling brown eyes and saw an assurance there which overcame all her objections. The knowledge that her father's machinations had been at work all along removed the last remaining scruples.

She nodded her head, unable to speak, and he gathered her in his arms and pressed her to him. Then, just as her happiness so overwhelmed her that she could scarcely stand it, his groom's voice sounded in her ear.

"I always fancied a bit of a go in the carriage with the mistress."

"Tom!" she shrieked, betraying her delight with a gurgle.

"Don't worry, my lady," he said pulling a forelock, but his voice was shaking. "It will be exactly as you please."

Harlequin Regency Romance™

COMING NEXT MONTH

#25 A SUSCEPTIBLE GENTLEMAN by Carola Dunn
Sarah Meade, sister of the vicar, had always loved
Adam Lancing, Viscount Cheverell. His charity work
had put him above reproach until he arrived at the
vicarage with three angry mistresses in tow. Having
rescued him from that coil, Sarah soon found herself
untangling him from three brand-new fiancées. If she
didn't laugh, she would cry, but first she would teach
him a lesson about love.

#26 LADY ELIZABETH by Linell Anston
Lady Elizabeth Croydon had waited three years for
Sir Antony Russellford to return from the Americas to
marry her. But having lost his fortune and self-esteem,
Tony insists that he cannot honour his pledge. While
Elizabeth makes it clear she will have no other, Tony
sets about to restore his fortune, though neither of
them could have guessed what the delay would
ultimately cost them.

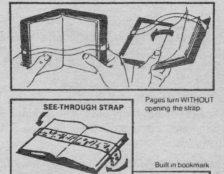

Have You Been Introduced To
THE GENTLEMAN
Yet?

If you enjoyed Dorothy Glenn's THE HELL RAISER (HH #45), you won't want to miss its companion book, THE GENTLEMAN, by Kristin James.

As a boy, Stephen Ferguson was taken away from his brother and his western home, then raised with all the comforts that money and city society could provide. As a man, he longed to be reunited with the family he'd nearly forgotten. In THE GENTLEMAN (HH #43) Stephen finds not only his father and brother but something even more precious—the love of a woman who is every inch his opposite—and absolutely his perfect match!